"Just a Human Being"

And Other Tales from Contemporary Cambodia

Edited by
Teri Shaffer Yamada

Nou Hach Literary Association: Translation Series, No. 1

Copyright © 2013 by Teri Shaffer Yamada. Permission to republish "Just a Human Being," "My Sister," and the "A Khmer Policeman's Story," first published in *Virtual Lotus: Modern Fiction of Southeast Asia*, granted by University of Michigan Press.

Cover art of *apsara* by Raksmey, associated with Daughters of Cambodia, an NGO that works to free sex-trafficked girls and assists them by providing safe housing and vocational training programs in Phnom Penh and other parts of Cambodia (www.daughtersofcambodia.org). Cover design with assistance of Kim Phally, Our Books.

No part of this collection can be reproduced or redistributed in any manner without written permission from the editor.

All proceeds from this book go to support the Nou Hach Literary Association's annual writers' conference in Phnom Penh. The Nou Hach Literary Association (http://nouhachjournal.net) is a non-profit NGO established in 1993 to support writers, literature, and literacy in Cambodia.

ISBN-13: 978-1482086355
ISBN-10: 1482086352

CONTENTS

ACKNOWLEDGEMENTS

Socially critical short fiction is a relatively new genre in Cambodia. The writers represented in this collection are at the forefront of experimental fiction in a country with a long history of censorship. A group of highly educated Cambodians—Khem Akhaing, Kho Tararith, Yin Luoth—and myself formed the translation team for most of these short stories. These are not direct translations but renditions created with the intent of maintaining the initial meaning of the text.

This collection would not have been possible without the support of John Weeks and his NGO Our Books in Phnom Penh. Finally, I would like to acknowledge other supporters whose contributions have made this publication possible: Ryan Paine, the Nou Hach Literary Association AsiaLink Intern for 2012, Madeline Dovale, Penelope Edwards, Jenna Grant, Laura Jean McKay, Monika Nowaczyk, Miranda Pen, John Singer, Matthew Trew, and Teresa Zimmerman-Liu. As a result of their assistance and the many supporters of the Nou Hach Literary Association, the first collection of Cambodian short fiction in English translation has come to fruition.

The Process of Promoting Khmer Literature

Yin Luoth

Yin Luoth is a founding member of the Nou Hach Literary Association and highly respected as a poet and fiction writer in Cambodia. This essay is reprinted from the Nou Hach Literary Journal, Vol. 2 (2005).

The Nou Hach Literary Association is named after a respected Cambodian writer, and its goal is to enable Khmer literature to progress and discover its own sense of modernity. Nou Hach stepped away from the old ways of writing drama, in verse with Buddhist concepts, to write a modern novel in narrative prose. His famous novel *A Withered Flower* was extremely moving for many readers and it is now in the standard high school curriculum. Nou Hach's masterpiece could not have come into existence without his intellectual capability and perseverance.

The Nou Hach Literary Association acknowledges that quality and considers him a role model: an ideal writer whom we will follow in order to reach our goals. Giving advice on how to foster ability, Niccolo Machiavelli, the Italian political philosopher of the fifteenth century, said: "Man should always walk in the path marked by great men and imitate those who have been preeminent, so that if his ability does not allow him to rise to their height, it may at least show some likeness to them." He also suggested that one should imitate the archer who pointed his arrow at the target and shot with all his might. If he hit the target, he could claim success; if not, at least he could come close.

Although the process of improving the quality of a person takes great patience and time, one has to start. Lao Tzu, the ancient Chinese philosopher said, "The journey of a thousand miles begins with the first step." In keeping with this concept, the Nou Hach Literary Association has taken a few significant first steps, such a organizing seminars, publishing books, broadcasting poems on the radio, television and radio interviews, and publishing articles in local magazines.

We realize that the steps we are taking may be different from those that Nou Hach took in the 1950s in both style and approach.

Our mission is to understand social reality and the true value of our society in the present time. We strongly believe that our success lies very much in the cooperation among Cambodian writers of all ages and social levels, both locally and abroad, and in cultivating support from scholars and foreign writers.

Short Fiction in Cambodia

Teri Yamada

Teri Yamada is a founding member of the Nou Hach Literary Association. She is a Professor of Asian Studies at CSU Long Beach.

During the era of European colonization, short fiction became a relatively popular genre in most of Southeast Asia. As print culture flourished due to better public education and increasing literacy from the end of the nineteenth century, short fiction became part of popular entertainment through inexpensive newspapers and magazines. And journalists became some of the most accomplished socially critical short fiction writers throughout the region. Like their counterparts elsewhere in the struggle against both colonial and post-colonial political oppression, fiction writers have been forced to negotiate state censorship. This has contributed to distinctive narrative forms of short fiction: coded content to avoid prison sentences and ensure that a story gets past the censor's critical gaze into print. Such techniques include allegories, animal tales, or stories historically framed in the distant past while actually dealing with current events. Even criticizing class injustices in contemporary Southeast Asian societies may create problems for a writer.[1] And this is certainly the case with fiction in Cambodia today.

Writers of modern short fiction in Cambodia have encountered more political and cultural barriers than their counterparts in other Southeast Asian nations. These obstacles have prevented or restrained the genre's popularity and development. Consequently, the short story in Cambodia remains a minor literature compared to the narrative sophistication of contemporary short fiction in other nations in Southeast Asia, such as Myanmar, Indonesia, Vietnam, Singapore and Thailand.[2]

A synergy of factors has contributed to Cambodia's unique situation of literary underdevelopment. This is partly due to a "conservative" cultural aesthetic traced to the early twentieth century (Edwards 2007).[3] This conservatism emerged from two factors: French colonial managers who valorized the "traditional" as a means to reify an "authentic" Cambodian cultural/national identity, and the reaction to French domination. Colored with anti-intellectual overtones, this conservative aesthetic has become unconsciously and deeply interwoven into the fabric of Cambodian public culture and discourse during the modern period. It is currently contested by popular youth culture in terms of nontraditional behaviors, musical tastes, and dress styles (Weinberger and Sam 2003).

Another historical factor that has contributed to the short story's literary underdevelopment in Cambodia is the comparatively delayed transfer of print technology. Due to different political conditions, the training of Cambodians in publishing and journalism took place in the 1930s compared to the early 1800s in Thailand, for example. The first Thai-language newspapers and journals, actually published by Thais, appeared in 1875 and 1876, compared to the mid-1930s in Cambodia when Cambodians first gained control of the publication process (Bee et al. 1989, 30). The popularity of the serialized modern novella and translations of Western and Chinese literature, which were published in Cambodian newspapers then, led to the novella (*pralomlok*) being the preferred form of modern entertainment literature in Cambodia, as it still is today.

State and self-censorship also contributed to short fiction's literary underdevelopment in Cambodia. Formal state censorship, a continuation of French colonial policy, was imposed during the post-independence period (1953–74). The near extinction of modern writers and literature occurred during the Pol Pot era (1975–79). Subsequently, there was the enforcement of socialist realism and state control of literary production during the People's Republic of Kampuchea (1979–89). Finally, the shadow of potential state censorship and violence since the 1990s continues to suppress unfettered creative expression. The five or six years after the United Nations Transitional Authority in Cambodia's successful national election in 1993 probably the most creative years for modern short fiction in Cambodian history. Many newspapers provided space for creative fiction in an atmosphere of free speech. By the late 1990s, however, the situation had changed. There were fewer independent newspapers and magazines. Censorship was regaining ground. Since then authors have to pay a fee to have their short fiction published.[4] Newspaper editors prefer more sensational short fiction with a penchant towards the pornographic (Lon Nara 2002). The era of the newspaper short story of imagination and depth appears to have already faded. Women's magazines still publish sentimental fiction in the form of serialized novels, often by women writers.

Although literacy rates have improved, most rapidly during the 1990s, they still significantly lag behind those in the rest of Southeast Asia with the exception of Laos. A culture of reading, which has never been established in Cambodia, is being superseded by the rapid emergence of a consumer culture enamored with visual and aural entertainment devices (video and compact disc players, MP3 downloads, cell phones, the "ring tone" phenomenon, etc.). This new consumer culture, with its desire for relatively expensive commodity goods, confronts an economy that requires the "typical" Cambodian to work several jobs in order to afford luxury goods on top of ordinary expenses. Middle-class professionals often work in various capacities at three or four different locations as part of their multiple-job income strategy. This means less time and incentive to read for entertainment even if it were considered a pleasurable past time.

Currently writers are eager to produce screenplays for television production since these are much more lucrative than novellas, still the most popular form of fiction in Cambodia. The wholesale pirating of writers' works, which occurs irrespective of the 2003 copyright law, also serves as a disincentive to writers, who already receive little monetary compensation for their creative work (Ryman 2006).[5] Or it leads to the mass authorship of similar novellas; some writers have publishing forty or more variations on a theme. These highly productive writers are considered "successful" although there is no critical discourse yet developed in Cambodia about "quality" literature. There is neither critical theory nor a book review genre. There still is no national distribution system for books so that an author could be assured that her works were available throughout the country. All of these factors form a silent conspiracy to inhibit literary development.

The stories in *"Just A Human Being" And Other Tales from Contemporary Cambodia* represent the best of socially critical short fiction in Cambodia. Many of them received Nou Hach literary awards between 2004 and 2009. Their themes include social "class" injustice or the deep division between a relative small number of wealthy Cambodians and the large number of tragically poor, or they explore the great divide between the urban and rural experience of modern life in Cambodia. Most of the stories are concerned with the greed and immorality of the modernity, decadence, crime and consumerism found in the urban culture of Phnom Penh or with the political payoffs available only to the Cambodian elite.

Many stories have a Buddhist subtext. "The Wallet," for example, reflects a Buddhist morality resonant with the traditional Cambodian folktale. As a contemporary morality tale it attempts to reify the Buddhist moral value of "compassion" and the law of karma. Karma and compassion are traditional values that many Cambodians feel have been lost since the Pol Pot era and the rush to acquire money and status in contemporary Cambodia. Several cautionary allegories in this collection have animals as characters. Phy Runn's "An Orphan Cat" reflects upon the cruelty and dis-engagement of many people in contrast to the kindness of just one man. Kao Seiha's "The Boat" (2006) involves a fisherman's family stranded at sea. At last they are discovered by a "foreign" boat, which refuses to help and waits until the distressed family is forced to sell its boat-home out of desperation. Instead of working together, the brothers fight over control of the boat as their father succumbs to illness. Ultimately "The Boat" is a story of multiple betrayals: the failure of trust and cooperation within the family leads to exploit-ation by "outsiders," who also cannot be trusted. There is treachery everywhere. Like "Lord of the Land," the inability of individuals within a group to cooperate under duress leads to the group's destruction.

Another type of short story published since the early 2000s contains a coming-of-age theme somewhat reminiscent of the so-cially critical literature of the 1940s in Cambodia. In Pen Chhornn's humorous "Obscure Way" (2006), the adolescent protagonist, a university student recently arrived in the big city from the countryside, encounters a series of unfortunate events following an atypical evening of fun at a disco, casino, and Karaoke bar. A recurrent theme in modern Khmer literature, our naïve rural lad gets taught a lesson in the big city. He has incurred a big hospital bill from being mugged on his only evening out. In order to repay this debt, he becomes a security guard at a wealthy politician's house. At this point the story devolves into a parody of corruption in contemporary Cambodia (Nissen 2006). Although our protagonist has lost his true love by the end of the story, he has gained a much deeper under-standing of contemporary society and himself. A similar theme occurs in Phy Runn's "An Orphan Cat" (2007). In this story a rural cat, befriended by a city cat, discovers that life is not so wonderful in Phnom Penh.

Finally, Phin Santel's example of expatriate writing, "The Revolver" (2006), is an English version of his Khmer short story "Katouch" (2005). In it the writer-protagonist leaves an attractive French lover and a life of luxury in France to return to Cambodia, tired of reconstructing memories of his homeland from books and photographs. As a writer, he feels compelled to create a great love story, to expand Cambodian literature, as he is tired of seeing only grim testimonial memoirs in the French bookstores. He finds this love story through an unanticipated encounter with some shady characters. It is ironic that today Phin Santel represents so many Cambodians who still feel they have no modern literature of great worth, echoing the concern of Cambodian writers in the late 1930s and 1940s.

ENDNOTES

1. For more information on Southeast Asian short fiction and its history see Yamada, 2002 and 2009.
2. For more information on Cambodian literature see Stewart and May. For an overview of short fiction in Southeast Asia see Yamada, 2009.
3. French policy in Cambodia emphasized the craft of reproduction rather than innovation in the arts and literature. Other comments about Cambodia as a conservative society "crushed by tradition" can be found in Martin 1994, 1–28.

4. For information on the media during this period, see Marston 1996, 208–42.
5. On the seriousness of copyright infringement and pirating in Cambodia, see International Intellectual Property Alliance 2007. In 2007, the Nou Hach Literary Group found pirated copies of Volume 1 of its journal and two CDs of its musical performances and radio programs being sold at various bookstalls and bookstores in Phnom Penh.

WORKS CITED

Amratisha, Klairung. 1998. "The Cambodian Novel: A Study of Its Emergence and Development." PhD Diss., School of Oriental and African Studies, University of London.

———. 2006. "The (Re-)emergence of Cambodian Women Writers at Home and Abroad." In *Expressions of Cambodia: The Politics of Tradition, Identity, and Change*, edited by Leakthina Chan-Pech Ollier and Tim Winter, 150–63. London: Routledge.

Bee, P. J., I. Brown, Patricia Herbert, and Manas Chitakasem. 1989."Thailand." In *South-East Asia, Languages and Literatures: A Select Guide*, edited by Patricia Herbert and Anthony Milner, 23–48. Honolulu: University of Hawai'i Press.

Edwards, Penelope. 2007. *Cambodge: The Cultivation of a Nation, 1860-1945*. Honolulu: University of Hawai'i Press.

Lon Nara. 2002. "The Unlucrative State of the Khmer Novel." *Phnom Penh Post,* Issue 11/07, 29 March-11 April.

Marston, John. 1996. "Cambodian News Media in the UNTAC Period and After." In *Propaganda, Politics, and Violence in Cambodia: Democratic Transition under United Nations Peace-Keeping*, edited by Steve Heder and Judy Ledgerwood 208-42. Armonk, NY: M. E. Sharpe.

Martin, Alexandrine. 1994. *Cambodia: A Shattered Society.* Berkeley: University of California Press.

Nissen, Christine. 2006. "Corruption Is 'Cool': Reflections on Bureaucratic Practices in Cambodia." *NIASnytt Asia Insights* (December) 3:18–19.

Ryman, Geoff. 2004. "Living Cambodia: A Look at Khmer Arts." Manuscript.

———. 2006. "Writing after the Slaughter: Geoff Ryman on Cambodian Writers." *Guardian*, 8 April.

Stewart, Frank, and Sharon May, eds. 2004. "In the Shadow of Angkor: Contemporary Writing from Cambodia." *Manoa* 16.1.

Weinberger, Evan, and Sam Rith. 2003. "Phat Times in Phnom Penh: Khmer Hip-Hop Takes the Rap at La Casa." *Phnom Penh Post,* 4–17 July.

Yamada, Teri Shaffer, ed. 2009. *Modern Short Fiction of Southeast Asia: A Literary History*. Ann Arbor: Association for Asian Studies.

———. 2002. *Virtual Lotus: Modern Fiction of Southeast Asia*. Ann Arbor: University of Michigan Press.

SHORT FICTION

1

An anonymous writer penned this experimental short story, which was published in a Phnom Penh daily newspaper in the 1990s. One way to avoid conflict as a writer of socially critical fiction is to remain anonymous. In "Just a Human Being" the author criticises the inhumanity of bureaucracy unless you happen to be an "important" person. A system of patron-client privilege is institutionalised in Cambodian social structure. The ballpoint pens mentioned in the story refer to the practice of important Khmer Rouge cadres who used these pens as a sign of their higher status during the Pol Pot era (1975–1979) when unauthorised writing was essentially prohibited. This short story's form is reminiscent of a short play or scene from a television drama. It was first published in Virtual Lotus: Modern Fiction of Southeast Asia, translation by John Marston.

Just a Human Being

Anonymous

Chief: Who's making such a commotion outside the door? What is that racket?

Assistant: There's a visitor demanding to meet you in person, sir.

Chief: How's that? Doesn't he know that I only receive visitors on Thursdays?

Assistant: Yes, he knows. But he says he has a matter of urgency, sir.

Chief: Then does he know that it's necessary to put his name down a month in advance?

Assistant: Yes. He more than knows; but he keeps pushing to come in.

Chief: God! What kind of person is this?

Assistant: He says he's just a human being.

Chief: But who is he? Who is he?

Assistant: All I can say is that he's just some person.

Chief: Very well. Then what does he look like, this variety of human being?

Assistant: There's nothing very special about him. He's wearing a grey shirt and trousers and has black shoes and a ragged captain's hat.

Chief: Ragged? And a captain's hat, no less? There's something unusual about that. What does he want, then? He doesn't say?

Assistant: No sir. He only insists on saying one thing: "I have an urgent matter; I'm just a human being who asks to meet with – "

Chief: He's not a little drunk and fuzzy, is he?

Assistant: No. His demeanour is quite focused and clear, sir.

Chief: Well, this is very strange. Certainly very strange. Hey, what do you think? Who is he?

Assistant: God in heaven knows. Shall I chase him away?

Chief: Don't rush things, now . . . just in case he might not just be a human being, but someone from the inspection committee.

Assistant: Could be or could not. The sleeves of his shirt are all worn through.

Chief: Why are you telling me about his worn through sleeves, then? *Focused and clear demeanour* —right on the day I don't receive visitors—*shirtsleeves worn through; just a human being*. I am very suspicious! There's something out of the ordinary here. Try to remember if you saw anything else.

Assistant: Anything else? In his pocket were clearly visible two ballpoint pens.

Chief: Two pens! Why didn't you tell me that right away?

(He unbuttons his shirt collar.)

Look at this clearly. Isn't this someone coming here under a pretext? And what reason is he coming here for?

Assistant: Here under a pretext? For what reason?

Chief: In order to inspect our way of working with the people, that's why.

Assistant: In that case, let me invite him to enter.

Chief: Wait a minute. We've got to do this right. Tell the secretary to make some coffee quickly and to bring out some cognac and other things like that as well. Pull the chairs together a little, here. And you can push the flowerpot away a little, there. Now go and invite him in and don't forget that you have to treat him very warmly and intimately, like a member of the family.

(The assistant comes back into the room soon after he has left.)

Chief: How's that? You're back already? Didn't you see him?

Assistant: He's there, sir. But there's one matter, which I thought I should come back and ask you about. He's weeping . . .

Chief: What? How do you mean, "He's weeping"?

Assistant: In the usual miserable way, with tears pouring from his eyes like drops of rain.

Chief: Is that so? Weeping. Then he must be just a human being after all. So then we try to . . . Ho, ho. Then everything is already quite in order. You can go kick his arse out of here, and you don't need to say anything to anybody. Tell the secretary that it's not necessary to make the coffee. As for the cognac, though . . . a stressful situation does strap one's energies. A human being, then . . . It's a problem we can handle by ourselves.

2

This short story, from a collection of short fiction by Sok Chanphal, was translated by Yin Luoth in 2009. Issues of corruption among local leadership, Khmer belief in dreams that in this case leads to tragedy, and the ongoing destruction caused by land mines associated with years of civil war and the Khmer Rouge are themes found in "Buried Treasure."

Buried Treasure

Sok Chanphal

Do you believe in dreams? I dreamt that someone told me to dig for a box of treasure! Maybe it wasn't a heavenly being who told me. Maybe it was a ghost, meandering about, who came to tease me.

This morning the sun is smiling at me showing its teeth. I am thinking about my dream last night: a box of gold buried on a hill under the palm trees. I have mixed feelings. I'm not too excited, but if I were to say that I am unconcerned that would be a lie. True. I have never thought that fortune would come to me easily. I'm fed up with my unfortunate life since childhood. Why would someone tell me during a sound sleep to dig for some treasure? Should it be a real box of gold, I wouldn't know how to use it being as ignorant as I am. The most I would do is buy food, eat and sleep, turning myself into a pig.

No matter what I think, I am walking toward the spot I saw in my dream. I walk with my mind full of doubt. The grass on the way looks like it has been trampled by oxen and cows; the ground looks like military horses have just passed through. No, it's not military horses or oxen and cows, it's villagers. I suddenly stop with my mouth open. Oh! Villagers are gathering under the palm trees making a noisy sound like sparrows arriving back at their nests in the evening. Looking at the crowd, I see black haired people right under the very palm trees that I saw in my dream.

Oh my goodness! I'm a little late. On the termite hill under the palm trees there really must be some buried treasure. Who has come to tell this to the villagers in their dreams?

"Hey, diggers have you seen any treasure yet?" A person who is standing beyond the crowd yells out; he won't get a chance to dig.

"Crash!" Don't be confused. It's not the sound of falling palm fruit; but the sound of two men fighting each other, and one of them has fallen down. Should palm fruit fall on them, it will cause lights to dance in their eyes.

"Hey, stop fighting! Evil has taken you over. You may not have a chance to share the treasure," an old lady yells. Those two stop fighting and come back to join the crowd.

Phang! A child cries. Everyone turns in the same direction. A policeman, who is acting like a big shot, is holding a handgun. He shoots up in the air, looks down and all around, then arrogantly commands: "Get off this termite hill right away! Back out!"

The villagers sound panicked when they see an old lady has fallen down.

Phang! Another sound of a gun shot. The villagers look at each other.

The policeman yells, "Don't mess up! Take this old lady away to her house. She is dying; no one is helping. Who is the child's mother?" The baby is crying noisily, "Take him away for feeding. This crowd is too rowdy. What do you mean, a buried treasure in the rice field? Go home right away!"

"We are not stupid enough to go! Do you plan to take this treasure yourself?" said a courageous young man.

Phang! The courageous young man turns blue. The policeman who used gun power yells again: "This is by order of the head of the commune. This is the last demand: Go home right away! Treasure or no treasure, leave it to the commune team. It is not yours. If it is real treasure, the head of the commune will report it up to the government office because it is a national treasure. They will bring money back for commune development."

All the villagers keep quiet, watching the National Working Group as they continue to dig according to their passion. The faces of the commune head and his wife show excitement the same way a gambler looks anticipating a win.

The village head shows up and smiles at the commune head who says, "If the head of the commune does not get involved, the villagers will fight to get a share, and it will be difficult to divide the treasure."

"Hey! If it's real treasure, I'll give you some. But is it true; is it real treasure?" The head of the village asks.

"Yes, it is certain. All the villagers had the same dream. I, my wife and my three children also dreamt it."

One of the villagers responds. "I wonder why all the villagers had the same dream?"

Oh! The villagers are still not going home. They are still wandering around the diggers. Each villager may think that the policeman doesn't have enough bullets to kill everyone. Should the policeman start shooting, he may kill somebody else first. As for me, I stand there and observe the people for awhile for my own self-satisfaction.

Suddenly, I see a metal box. I hear a shout from the head of the commune: "Bring it up; let me open it myself."

The villagers squeeze in to see the head of the commune open the box. I think to myself, *Let it be. Treasure or no treasure, there are so many people. I don't think I deserve to share any part of it.* I walk back home indifferently, having left the vicinity for about three minutes.

Kreang! It was not a gunshot, my ears tell me, but the sound of a land mine explosion.

3

"An Orphan Cat" won third place in short fiction at the Nou Hach Literary Competition, 2007. It was published in Nou Hach Literary Journal, Vol. IV (2007) and translated by the Nou Hach Literary Association translation team. This story contains several recurrent themes found in new socially critical fiction in Cambodia: the divide between an urban and rural lifestyle, with the opportunity and excitement big city life represents for rural folk. Cats are the protagonists in this tale. Animal stories play an important part in Cambodian didactic folktales, specifically the Judge Rabbit series; however, this writer uses animals in a modern way to express cruelty and lack of compassion in contemporary Cambodian society. The character Mr Jeff in this story refers to British writer Geoff Ryman, author of The King's Last Song, who came to Cambodia in 2006 and gave a short story workshop for Khmer writers.

An Orphan Cat

Phy Runn

It's been three years now since I lost contact with my older sister. Before my mother passed away, my sister told me that I could find her in Phnom Penh. But, gosh, I don't know anything about that city so I wonder how I could possibly find her?

My friend Atrasak is living with a foreigner in Phnom Penh. Whenever his owner goes anywhere, he goes along. This owner is always giving Atrasak a bath. He gives him the best food and makes sure Atrasak gets vaccinations to stay healthy. My life is different. I live with Cambodians in the countryside. Although I've lived with this family for a long time, they have never taken care of me. Instead they hit me so I'll go away. When they roast fish, I can hardly stand it.

Currently I'm very distraught about my mother's death. I keep wondering why she had to die. The answer is simply because there was no food for her in this house. She always was able to find something to eat outside until she got sick, that is until she got caught in the mousetrap that ultimately killed her. When my mother died, my younger siblings weren't even able to walk yet. The owner of the house just tossed them out.

This past year has been a very sad time for me due to my mother's death and lost siblings. I really wonder why I'm such an unlucky cat. My younger brother is now separated from me and I have no idea of his whereabouts. My older sister is in Phnom Penh and there has been no news of her. I really don't know if she is well or not. Now with just my older sister left, I'm really going to dedicate myself to finding her.

Phnom Penh.

Now Atrasak and Mr Jeff have brought me to Phnom Penh with them. Atrasak has shown me all the places he knows here. I've experienced the palace garden, cinemas, Independence Monument, Wat Phnom, Phnom Penh International Airport, the golf courses, supermarkets, and even the slaughter houses, which really scared me.

I'm really healthy now because I've been living in an air-conditioned home and eating delicious food like hamburger and tapioca pearl tea every day.

Being in the city makes me happy. Sometimes I get angry about my older sister who has been living so happily in this city but didn't bother to bring our mother to live with her. Until the day she died my mother was always worried about my sister. If I happen to meet sister, I'm really going to get angry.

Atrasak and I are always happy. I've stopped thinking about my older sister since she has nothing to worry about in Phnom Penh.

Tonight I want to go out for a walk so I ask Atrasak to go with me. I want to know what it's like at night in this city. We leave very quietly without telling Mr Jeff, without even making the dog bark.

The cool, fresh evening air along the road is making us sleepy.

"Where should we go now?" I ask Atrasak.

"Follow me!" he replies. "My friend, it's so easy to stroll around Phnom Penh at night since few people are walking on the road. Follow me carefully, though, because the cars go very fast."

We talk about all sorts of things, the stars and the moon. The moon in the countryside and the city is beautiful in both places—the moonlight is the same. This sameness is not the case for country and city cats. In the city there is money and delicious food. In the countryside, the cats are poor, skinny, and beaten daily by their owners.

"Everything in heaven is wonderful!" Atrasak exclaims.

"Have you been to heaven?" I ask him, thinking I might like to go there.

"I've just seen it on TV," Atrasak replies, "but someday I'd like to ask Mr Jeff to take me there."

"Don't forget to take me," I say.

Just as I am deeply absorbed in the beauty of the moonlight, I hear someone cry out. "Help! Help me!"

"What's the matter?" I shout as I jump on a roof to see what's happening. Oh my! There is a gang of male cats having sex with one unwilling female. They are telling her, "My dear, don't try to run away. Now you have a choice: pleasure or death!"

The female cat Prapeh doesn't reply but just meows pitifully, wanting someone to help her. She finally chooses to jump from the roof in order to escape. The leader of the male cats Akmao, the biggest among them, says, "Don't go after her, she's chosen death."

I peer down at her as she dies in the alley below, so pitiful.

"What do you think about this?" I ask Atrasak.

"Everything in Phnom Penh is not the way you think it is," he replies. "We have good luck because we live with a kind owner, but all these cats have no one to take care of them. They don't have anyone to give them advice, they don't have any place to stay. Every day they must search for a safe place to rest. They don't have enough food and sometimes the big rats kill them. Oh my friend, you will learn more about this city and what happens here. Let me tell you that I nearly died in Phnom Penh when I was just three months old."

"What happened?" I ask him.

"At that time I didn't know what happened to my mother. I had five brothers and sisters. They died one by one because of dogs, lack of food, car accidents, falling from trees, or people killing them." He speaks so sadly.

And as for me, I have no idea how to cross a road. What to do? Where to go? It is hard for me to keep listening to Atrasak's sad story.

"You understand," he continues, "in Phnom Penh the traffic lights are not so good. I had to avoid bicycles, motorcycles, and all kinds of vehicles on the road. I could die at any time. The motorcycles and vehicles drive very fast and don't care about my life. I felt so very tired and just closed my eyes, waiting to die on the street, but one car came to a stop right over me. The owner got out of the car, picked me up, and took me with him."

"What happened next?" I ask.

"He helped me."

"Okay, so who was the kind person?" I ask.

"It was Mr Jeff. We live with him now."

"Pondering this, I think the lives of all animals are much the same. Their problems are similar, although there are a few lucky animals like you. There aren't very many kind-hearted people like Mr Jeff. Oh, I want to thank you for letting me live with you."

"Don't thank me," Atrasak replies, "thank Mr Jeff. We are both cats so I can't help you. If Mr Jeff had seen Prapeh, the cat who just died, she wouldn't be dead now. Okay, I'm taking you to the market now."

"Maybe the market is closed," I say.

"The supermarket never closes in the city. But if it is closed, I'll take you to visit a Karaoke bar or we can go dancing. I know about all these things so don't worry. Tonight, I have lots of money. I'll pay for you so you'll be happy."

The supermarket is very noisy with cheerful people and happy pets. The German Shepherds and cats are eating a lot at the Suki soup place and the hamburger shop. As for me, the doctor said I should diet due to high cholesterol. Artrasak is also dieting. We talk happily about our memories as we wander about the supermarket.

"I can't forget about when I was poor," said Atrasak. "I must divide what I have and give it to the poor and hungry. Don't you think so? Our cat ancestors certainly weren't able to take gold or money to heaven with them when they died."

"That's so," I say, "but why do we bite each other then, to get more money?"

"Because we've lost our morality and virtue," he answers. "Everyone is always thinking about how to get lots of money. But when money comes first, there's no peace in life. Think about Mr Jeff. He tries to work for everyone. Every day we see someone who needs his help to do this or that for society. He doesn't do any of this to get money but just thinks about humanity."

"We are lucky to live with a wise person," I say. "We can follow his example. But there are a million cats living in the countryside and the city that are unlucky like we used to be."

"Sure, like Apopel last year."

"Who is Apopel?" I ask.

"A cat who always was asking for food."

"What happened to him?"

"His owner used to be a powerful man who could do whatever he wanted and made everyone afraid. Apopel was just like him. He wanted all the beautiful female cats. He bit everyone. Sometimes he would just take someone's dried fish and leave because his powerful owner protects him. But when his owner went to prison, all his owner's possessions were confiscated, so Apopel had nothing. Even now no one feels sorry for him, because when he lived with a powerful man, he didn't help anyone. For example, instead of giving away his leftover food to the needy, he just set it aside and let it rot."

"Let's not talk anymore," I say. "Let's go back home."

"Okay, let's go. Maybe Mr Jeff is looking for us."

The road home was very dark since it was about to rain. A car was swerving on the road, then we heard a loud bang. Oh my god! The car hit a light pole and bounced off, hitting us both and crushing my two back legs. I shout "Atrasak! Atrasak!" but there is no reply. I start shouting for anyone to help. There are many cats around me, but no one comes to our aid.

It rains at midnight as I try to protect Atrasak, licking his pitiful body. Why did my friend have such a short life? Oh that drunkard, why was he so cruel? You have a car, why drive it to kill others. You have no compassion.

I start crying because I feel so sorry about my friend. Many cats are coming to see why I'm in tears. I ask them for help but there is no response. They leave one by one. I cry alone. When my mother died, I cried just a little; when Atrasak died, I cried a lot. I can't stop thinking about him. I feel so sorry about his short life. No one knows about the life of cats.

Atrasak is dead. His body is stiff and motionless on the road. It breaks my heart every time a motorbike or car drives over him again. No one has the compassion to stop and pick him up off the street. They wish him dead again and again when they drive over his body and get splashed with his blood. I'm so sorry that I can't help you Atrasak. You can see that I've been yelling for help but no one has come.

All that arises ultimately ceases, but just make sure that your life isn't ended by a drunk driver! We aren't bad. We don't steal. So why doesn't anyone help us? I'm weak as I start crawling to the Frangipani tree. The fragrance of its flowers doesn't attract me as I keep gazing at Atrasak. I'm thinking about my life.

My mother's request, before her death, was to find my older sister. Oh sister! If I'd met you, perhaps you would not have permitted me to go for a walk late at night. My sister would have stopped me just like my mom. And she would have told me, "Don't bite people!" Mother! Phnom Penh is different from our countryside home. How can I find my sister? I apologise to you that I haven't been able to find her.

There are so many people driving noisily on the road. I'm still bleeding and it's making me so faint.

I hear the sound of crickets nearby and it wakes me. Atrasak is nowhere in sight. Oh no! I think someone has taken him somewhere for food. I turn to the right and see the street cleaners. Maybe they put him in the bin, so I try to crawl rapidly across the road to the trash bin. It reeks with a horrendous odour and is covered with flies. There are many poor people eating out of the trash bin as if the food they found there is most delicious. Oh the destiny of sentient beings born in this world! Why are so many of them unlucky? I really want to live, to learn more about a cat's life in this world. I'm crying out, wanting someone to take Atrasak's body out of the bin, but nobody comes to assist me.

Help! It's a dog. Some French dog is trying to bite me, but its owner doesn't even notice. The owner stands there doing nothing as the dog attempts to hurt me. I'd like to bite both the owner and his dog, but I'm crippled and can't. Many cats have come to smell the bin and left. They don't care about my appeals for help. "Find someone else to help you," they say. "I can't. I'm busy looking for food. If I help you, I might end up hungry like last night."

Yesterday I thought this city was a very rich and happy place. I guessed that my older sister must be living with some wealthy woman here, not caring about my mother and me. But everything has changed now. Just this morning many dogs and cats have come to find discarded food in the bin, and many poor people are collecting junk plastic to sell. It is harder to live in the city than the country. In the city no one knows me. If this happened to me in the countryside, maybe someone would have helped.

Mr Jeff, perhaps you are worried about Atrasak and me. Maybe you blame me. I know that if I hadn't come here, Atrasak wouldn't have left the house. Perhaps you feel sorry that he brought me to live with you, Mr Jeff. I'll accept all your blame. I accept everything that you think about a cat like me.

The next morning arrives and I'm aware of bandages on my legs. I feel sick and my body aches. Mr Jeff! I'm seeing Mr Jeff! He is slowly petting me and smiling. I understand how he feels about me and I reach out to touch him with my front paw. I want to tell him about everything that's happened to me. I want to say I'm sorry but I can't speak. I just cling to him and lick his hand. I show how grateful I am.

That night the doctor arrives to look at my legs again. After that I see him carrying Atrasak past me in a plastic bag. I can see Mr Jeff's tears, and I start crying again, too.

4

"The Wallet" won third place in short fiction in the Nou Hach Literary Competition, 2009. It was published in Khmer with an English translation by Heng Kanitha in the Nou Hach Literary Journal, Vol. VI (2009). The gap between rich and poor in Cambodia and the arrogant tendency of the wealthy to belittle those socially below them, especially the working poor who may be trapped in poverty, is a theme found in many of the other short stories in this collection along with the importance of reclaiming the Buddhist value of compassion.

The Wallet

Sok Chanphal

My friends call at work telling me to hurry up and meet them. Leaving in my car, I see a bloody body on the street right outside the hospital entrance. I roll down my car window and a woman yells, "Doctor, please help! Someone hit him. It's very serious, a hit-and-run."

I stare at the bloody body again, then roll up the window and drive away. There is a saying that only poor people think of other poor people. This incident is an example. The three or four people who notice the man on the street are only poor people who live near the hospital. It appears that the old man who got hit is a beggar who walks around pretending to be blind. It must be his karmic retribution for acting that way.

I park my car carefully and walk into a pub pondering the shortness of life. How do we find meaning in it? Working as a doctor, I've learned that life is birth and death. In just my hospital alone babies are born and old men die in the same moment. The only job we have in life is to find joy that gives us happiness.

I drink some good wine and sit close to a pretty girl. Who says that angels are happier than men on earth?

"Did you drop your wallet, sir?" Asks a girl.

I see a girl selling jasmine flowers approaching me with my wallet. I glance at her face and take the wallet to make sure nothing has been taken . . . she quickly walks away from me and I wonder why.

"Wait," I say.

She turns, asking, "Sir, do you want to buy my flowers?"

I nod my head indicating that I do and she comes back. I stare at her not thinking about the price of jasmine flowers. I want to understand her feelings so I ask, "Why didn't you take my wallet and run home?"

She looks at me curiously and says, "Because it's yours."

"Do you know how much money there is in this wallet?" I ask.

She shakes her head.

"The money in here would allow you to stop selling flowers and be independent for a year."

The girl looks at me with a blank face.

"Do you regret not taking it?" I ask her.

"No, sir. I like selling flowers. I don't want to stop."

I simultaneously want to laugh and cry at this stupid girl. I take 50,000 riels from my wallet and give it to her.

"One flower garland is only 1,000 riels."

"Take it. It's for you."

"But, my mother and father would not allow me to accept this anyway," she says.

"It is your gift for returning my wallet."

The girl shakes her head. "I only picked up your wallet. It was no trouble. Why give me all this? My mother and father tell me, 'People must help each other so that everyone can be happy'."

I laugh, shaking a bit.

"Who are your parents?" I ask her. "Are they monks and nuns?"

"My father is a construction worker and my mother sells vegetables in the market place."

I remain silent because I feel troubled by what she says.

She notices and continues talking, "My father and mother Always advise me, 'Helping people is natural for humans.' I am happy to pick up your wallet. If you'd lost your wallet, you would have been unhappy. My mother and father also tell me, 'Taking care of other people uplifts your spirit too. You must help others just as you would help yourself.'"

I think what stupid parents to make their child stupid, too, and say to her, "Your father and mother advise you that doing good brings good, right?"

"Yes, my father and mother say that greedy people do bad things. There are not many greedy people who do good things. Actually, though, doing good is not hard."

This girl is only parroting the words of her parents. I ask her parents' questions by asking them through her.

"So far, what have your family's good deeds yielded?"

"I haven't seen anything yet."

I laugh and say, "Doesn't doing good bring good?"

"My parents say if you do good for a reason, it isn't doing good."

I keep silent thinking, "Our home is our first school. With unsuccessful parents who are construction workers and vegetable sellers, where do they get any wisdom to guide their child?"

Seeing my silence, the girl begins to walk away, but I stop her.

"What would you like to be in the future? Do you want to walk around selling flowers forever?"

She thinks for a second, and answers, "My parents tell me that all work is good if people are good themselves. My father builds homes for people to live in, and my mother sells vegetables for people to cook for meals. And when I am not in school, I sell flowers to earn money to help my mother and father."

Bad people take advantage of good people. People like this girl's parents must have been stepped on until they are the sad people they seem to be now.

"Don't you all want some things?" I ask her.

"My father and mother tell me, 'Virtuous things are what we need most.' We need to learn how to be virtuous."

It seems that being too virtuous always leads to poverty. The girl walks away. She must be thinking all the time about doing virtuous things so she can tell her parents. She is the one person in a million who thinks like this. The builder remains a builder because he is full of virtue. I am happy to give this wallet to you. People who are greedy do bad things. Doing good things for a reason is not doing good. We must live to learn to be virtuous. All work has value, even selling vegetables.

How funny, even to me, a doctor.

I think of her and laugh. I didn't think that the words of a little girl selling flowers would bring me to a standstill. I look around the pub thinking where I might find happiness in my life. My friends, still waiting for me, must be curious about what's happened. All of us will laugh until I forget all my worries. But, I turn around to go back.

I drive quickly to the hospital. The bloody man is still lying on the ground. Doctors are truly greedy people who do bad things. But who is a stupid person like the girl who picks up my wallet and doesn't want anything in return?

I tell the doctors to quickly operate on the wounded man. They must be wondering who will pay for the operation? Or will they merely do the operation as quickly as possible?

I begin to operate on the man's leg so that in the future he will be able to walk like me. As I am operating on the man, I feel a sense of freedom that comes from the desire to help another. I'm still thinking of the flower girl's words, filling me with understanding a little bit at a time until my heart is now full.

Finally, the operation is successful. This is the first time I've been happy doing my job. A builder is a builder. I've heard those words before, but now I understand their significance. I think of the man's family. They will be happy that their husband, father, or brother continues to be in their lives. This is what makes me happy.

I leave the hospital to return home. On the way, I see the girl who sells flowers walking with an older woman who must be her mother. I stop the car, walk over to her and ask, "Where are you going?"

The girl and her mother look at me with tearful eyes. She says, "My father hasn't come home since sunset. We are worried that he has fainted or been in an accident."

I am surprised. I take them to see the man I have just helped. The girl and her mother run to hug him, his face is covered in tears.

I, too, cry uncontrollably. The three of them turn to me, looking as if I were a god.

I tell them, "I should be the one to thank you."

I realize there is nothing that feels better than doing good. There is nothing that excites me more than having this realization. Doing good really does yield good. If that girl hadn't returned my wallet, she probably would have lost her father forever.

5

Yur Karavuth was a staff writer for Pracheachon newspaper when this story was published in 1991. It illustrates the satirical use of fiction in Cambodian newspapers in the early 1990s, the main venue of publication for this genre. Since the UNTAC era, freedom of the press and free speech have become important issues for many Cambodians. In a climate of violence, it seems safer to criticize political, military, and police corruption though the medium of fiction, especially if it is in the form of satirical humor. "A Khmer Policeman's Story: A Goddamn Rich Man of the New Era" also illustrates a culture of dubious acquisition and speculation that continues to plague the social development of contemporary Cambodia. This short story, translated by John Marston and Kheang Un, was first published in Virtual Lotus: Modern Fiction of Southeast Asia (2002).

A Khmer Policeman's Story: A Goddamn Rich Man of the New Era

Yur Karavuth

Don't laugh or cry at my story: it is merely the way the hand of fate has marked my present incarnation. Here in the police department, I have many friends who like to joke around with me. They have all given me a nickname: "the goddamn rich man of the new era". Well, of course, it's very appropriate.

In 1988 I sold a small villa of mine for 40 *domlong*. My god! As you know already, at that time 40 *domlong* was quite a sum of money. When they heard, the faces of my wife and children blossomed like a mint seed in water.

Once we had the 40 *domlong* in our hands, my wife and I began thinking hard—like the boy in the Cambodian story who thinks so hard that he falls out of the sugar palm tree.

We thought about it during the day as we rested and dreamt about it at night while we slept. It was truly thinking on a major scale because we realized there would be a portion of money left over after buying an apartment, which we could use as capital for doing business with the best of them.

So, dreaming of this and dreaming of that, we bought an apartment for 25 *domlong*, leaving 15 *domlong*. Then after giving some to various relatives— five *domlong*, all told—there was 10 *domlong* left to put in the pot of the *tong tin* lending-group schemes at the Orasey Market.

This course of action was in part motivated by thinking that I didn't want to trouble my wife by setting up a business where she would have to work—better to keep her white, soft, and lovely for her husband, right?

I put in two *domlong* here and one there. I started out putting in five *chi* in four places and ended up putting five *chi* in ten places. It was great fun spending it from day to day, just waiting for the interest to roll in.

It was a delicious way of life for almost a year—until the guy holding the pot skipped town and the tong tin house went bust, creating a very sorry situation indeed.

Whoever I talked to—the tong tin head or the other members of the lending group—repeated the same story, one version like another all stuck together like shrimp in a glob of shrimp paste. The sum of money, every bit of it—more than 10 *domlong*—had been thrown away neatly!

Suddenly not only my mother-in-law, but my own mother and all my other relatives in chorus, laid the blame 100 per cent on me!

They ask, "How were you playing *tong tin* so that you ended up losing the money?"

When I was doing well by the scheme, I thought to myself, I never heard a word of criticism. Only when misfortune falls do they band together and blame me.

Nonetheless, by the middle of 1989—oh my god, a goddamn rich man of the new era like myself was still getting along in high style. That year someone came by who wanted to buy my 25 *domlong* apartment and was so bold as to offer 35 *domlong*. I discussed the offer with my wife.

"Shall we sell it again, sweetheart?" I ask her.

"It's completely up to you, dear," she says.

I love my wife because when I ask her about something, she always says it's up to me. It's things like this that mean I could never be false to her love.

Sometimes, when it is her time of month—what we call her "vacation time"—she will say to me straightforwardly: "Dear, when I have to behave modestly like this, I'm afraid it leaves you bored and restless, doesn't it?" Well, this is what they call a wife who understands her husband...

Let me make something clear at this point. Having been on the police force for 13 or 14 years, I can boast a little. When it comes to "being on the take"—a present here for a favor there, skimming a little off the top or skimming a little off the bottom, tucking something away for a rainy day—there hasn't been any of that.

For a goddamn rich man of the new era like myself, the only source of wealth is selling houses. So when I talk about my wife's willingness to do what I decide, you should understand that she agrees because she knows that whatever I do will be honest.

I decided to sell the apartment for the price offered to me. I lost no time in buying another house for 20 *domlong*, leaving 15 *domlong* to buy a Toyota Corona for my wife and children to drive, with a little left over for the pleasures of life.

It is a human thing that when you have a car you want to show off. And it is precisely because of this car that they gave me the nickname, "the goddamn rich man of the new era". My wife and children were truly happy: a car to drive like the best of them!

But by the end of 1990 the money was gone, my wife was sick, and the car had broken down. Health gone, peace of mind gone, and no money to boot! I decided to sell the car. Since I needed the money quickly, I sold the car for five *domlong,* losing two *domlong*. I used most of the money for the medical bills; the rest went for family expenses.

By the time New Years rolled by in 1991, the economic situation was beginning to bubble and boil. A playboy type came by offering to buy my apartment. This time the offer was 30 *domlong*. I decided to sell. Wealth again! I went out with my wife and got a 15 *domlong* apartment. With the money left over, we bought a piece of land just east of the city. It was great! Having bought the land, there was enough money to buy a car, too! Every Sunday I would go with my wife and the kids to look at the land.

As luck would have it, one of the suburbanites there got the mistaken idea that I was a rich businessman. Suddenly, at the end of 1991, the lid blew off of things, and the guy said I had bought land that belonged to him. He would not allow it. Well, since the other guy was higher up than me, and I was afraid, also, because I heard he had connections in even higher places, I surrendered pretty quickly—losing the match before I'd even entered the ring.

My wife cried a lot at that time, as though she were in great pain. She consoled me, saying, "Oh, sweetheart, don't be angry about fate: don't complain about what has been allotted in life. Don't struggle with a piece of rock; you will only end up wounding yourself."

I did at least get two *domlong* out of the settlement. In the end, I decided to sell that last apartment, too, for 25 *domlong*. This is as far as I can go, I thought to myself—the only course left for me is to buy land in the country so I will have the means of earning a living.

My wife and I decided that she and the kids would go live in a wood house on a medium-size piece of farmland. We sold the car to meet the needs of my wife, and especially, of the kids who were bigger by now.

So this is my story—from living in a stone house with brick columns on its own plot of land, I progressed to a spacious apartment. And from there I moved on to a small, rather crowded apartment. Finally, I ended up in the sticks enjoying the fresh air.

I do know, though, that it's not just me, a poor policeman, who has a story like this. I suspect there are others who've received the nickname “a goddamn rich man of the new era,” because of experiences like my own.

6

"The Boat" won second place in short fiction at the Nou Hach Literary Competition, 2006. It was published in both Khmer and English translation in the Nou Hach Literary Journal, Vol. 3. One interpretation of "The Boat" is that it embodies a national allegory symbolizing the insecurity that many Cambodians have experienced since French colonial times: the fear that their valuable property is being given away by the French to neighbouring nations or absorbed by stronger, duplicitous "outsiders" during a time of political weakness. Like the short story "Lord of the Land," it also portrays the destructive selfishness of an individual family member more concerned with himself than other family members. This story may be a commentary on Cambodians as a national family. Internal strife, the kind that so many Cambodians experienced during the Khmer Rouge era (1975-79), destroyed many families while dismantling the country's own material and intellectual infrastructure.

The Boat

Kao Seiha

The sun is setting now and the sky is filled with a golden glow. The horizon is ablaze, a rosy red, reflecting brilliantly off the sea. Seagulls cover the sky as they return home for the evening.

There is a family on shore quickly preparing for a night of fishing. This family lives on a boat; working as fishermen enables them to eat. Although this occupation provides them with food, it is very dangerous work.

Mr Sieun's boat is the best. Inherited from his grandparents, it is made of top-quality wood and decorated on the sides with a painted dragon snake and Garuda. It has an outboard motor to help them fish. Everybody likes this boat and wants to own it. A number of foreigners would like to purchase it, but Mr Sieun refuses to sell.

Now this family is preparing to depart. Mr Sieun and his two sons, Saarieun and Sarin, push the boat out to sea while Mingsaat and Sreipou, his wife and daughter, prepare the nets for fishing. Mr Sieun is a strong man, determined and argumentative, with curly hair receding in the front, thin eyelashes and lips. He is strong minded and opinionated, never listening to anyone's advice. He always acts as the boss of the family and demands that things go his way.

"Little Rieun," he says to his son, "give me the scull so I can push off and start the motor."

Saarieun passes the scull to his father, who steers the boat skilfully due to his years of experience and lifetime of living on the boat. The sound of the motor follows them out to sea and over the waves to their destination.

The sky turns dark with ominous clouds while they are still fishing. They can't see anything, not even light from the stars and moon. Mingsaat has prepared dinner and calls to her husband and children. He secures the fishing gear and goes to eat with them.

That night the wind is much stronger than usual. Mr Sieun peers out to sea trying to understand the weather conditions, and looks worried. Soon it starts to rain in torrents fed by a furious wind, making them all afraid. The waves are pounding the boat, taking them far from their original destination. The wick of the boat lamp has blown out, engulfing them in darkness.

Mr Sieun is stronger than the rest of them. He sits at the bow observing the situation while his two sons sit at the stern trying to control the motor. Mingsaat and their daughter are frightened, praying that all will go well.

The powerful waves batter the boat as the salty water starts pouring over the sides. Mingsaat and Sreipou stop praying and start bailing the boat as it tips from side to side, buffeted by the waves and wind. They have never been so frightened. Finally the intensity of the storm lessens and they are no longer so afraid, but none of them know where they are. Mr Sieun looks around and becomes very worried.

Then the motor quits. Mr Sieun tells his son to take the fuel and fill the engine, but the motor still won't start.

Not far from their location is another boat and Mr Sieun attempts to get their attention by shouting for help. "Oh, brother," he yells, "please help me and take us to land!"

"I can't help you," the owner of the other boat replies in a foreign accent, difficult to understand. "My boat is too slow."

Mr Sieun attempts to ask another boat to help them, but no one will come to his aid. He gets really angry. They haven't been able to fish and now they will have to scull helplessly somewhere.

Many days have passed. Mr Sieun's boat has been drifting at sea. They have no idea what will happen to them. Then another foreign boat approaches and moves alongside. Its owner discusses various innocuous things, then asks about buying the boat. This foreigner has asked to buy Mr Sieun's boat many times before, but he has refused to sell. Now Mr Sieun offers to sell one of their sculls.

Mingsaat has been listening while repairing a fishing net. "Why, husband, did you offer to sell a scull? Don't do that. I don't agree with your plan. We need both sculls for the boat. We can't go anywhere without the scull!"

Mr Sieun responds in anger, "It's none of your business, stupid wife! We have to sell it for water, rice, some fish or meat. Or do you just want to die? We have two sculls; there is no problem if we sell one. Don't worry so much, stupid, I know what I'm doing!"

Mingsaat kept silent while caressing the scull to show her regret. After her husband passes the scull to the foreign boat, it moves away.

The wife of the foreign boat's owner then angrily accosts her husband, "You! Why did you exchange our food for this scull? What interest do you have in it?"

Smiling, her husband strokes the scull and responds, "They are going to get stuck. Today they sold their scull to us. Tomorrow we will force them to sell the other one. After that they will have to sell the boat to us. We've wanted to buy their boat for a long time. I'm sure this will be a good opportunity for us. Now Mr Sieun's boat is floating like seaweed on the ocean. They can't find their way to shore. Everything is going our way. This plan will succeed. We must watch them carefully. When this family gets stuck, it becomes a good opportunity for us." They smile and laugh.

Now Mr Sieun's luck is coming to an end. He is worried. They are not catching any fish and are trying to move their boat across the sea with just one scull and no motor. Everything has been difficult. His stomach problems have worsened, making him very ill, and their food supply is running out. All this makes the owner of the foreign boat very happy.

Mr Sieun has his way even when he is ill. He thinks that no one can do the job the way he can because the children are so young and don't have enough experience with sculling the boat. But Mr Sieun and his family have lost their way. They can't see the shoreline or find an island. This is causing them to despair, especially Mr Sieun. Now he is so sick that he can't even steer the boat. His illness has overtaken him; he is unable to move so he tells his two sons to take over the boat.

After the father has authorised Saarieun and Sarin to take over, they begin to quarrel loudly over who gets the remaining scull.

"Give it to me!" Saarieun demands. "You are younger and you don't know the direction."

"Brother, let me use the scull!" demands Sarin. "I'm younger but I'm also stronger than you are."

Their fighting makes the boat rock back and forth, letting water flow in over its sides.

Sreipou shouts at her brothers, "Stop it! Stop fighting! You never think about helping; you just argue. Brother, you have shamed us. Look! The people on the foreign boat are laughing at you. They don't want to help us, but they are willing to laugh at our expense. Please stop it. Don't make them look down on us."

They listen to her. Sarin stops fighting with Saarieun, and turns to the foreign boat, shouting, "What are you looking at us for? Haven't you seen anybody fight before? Huh, you are pirates violating borders."

A whole day passes while Saarieun steers the boat, but they don't see any land. Night arrives.

Sreipou says to Saarieun, "Brother, if we keep going in this direction, we aren't going to find land, because I remember we need to follow this star." She points toward a star shining in the night sky.

Saarieun turns to her and replies. "Stop talking; you are a girl. You should be thinking about cooking and helping mother. I know what I'm doing; don't tell me what to do."

Hearing this, she looks down, becoming depressed about expressing an opinion. Then her mother intervenes, saying to her son, "You should be more modest, Saarieun. Don't talk like that to your sister. She's just trying to help us find land. You know there is a proverb: 'Two heads are better than one.' You don't understand the limits of your capability. You need to give some responsibility to your siblings. That would be good."

"How can I share responsibility," Saarieun asks while glancing at Sarin, "if they don't know how to use the scull well?"

"And what about you?" Sarin yells. "You think you are so much better than me."

Mingsaat interjects, "You are brothers, don't talk like this to each other. Don't quarrel."

Saarieun and Sarin keep quiet as she continues, "We are destined to live together on this boat. We don't know the way to shore, and we've encountered adversity at sea—storms, heavy rain, huge waves, and not enough food. And through all of this, none of the other boats have helped us. They always gave us false directions. Now you must do the right thing and do something to find land. Stop quarrelling. You must work together."

Saying this, she anxiously feeds her husband some rice porridge. Saarieun and Sarin glare at each other and keep silent, but their demeanour shows that they both still want to steer the boat.

The weather is unpredictable. Suddenly a storm rises; gusts of wind and huge waves batter the boat making it unstable. But Sarin is doing nothing while everyone else is busy keeping the boat afloat.

Saarieun starts yelling at Sarin, "You, Sarin! Why aren't you helping us bail the boat? The water is pouring in and we are sinking!"

"You said you were strong and could do anything," Sarin replies. "Please do it, since I'm not capable according to you."

Saarieun keeps silent and tries to bail the boat himself. Sarin finally decides that the situation has become too serious and decides to help. Mr Sieun has just lost consciousness when the foreign boat appears. Everyone in Mr Sieun's boat begs them for help.

The owner of the foreign boat says, "I can help you, on one condition."

"What's that?" asks Saarieun.

"If we help your family, you must give me your boat."

They glance at each other reluctantly.

The owner of the foreign boat assesses the situation and continues speaking, "Please decide; it's your boat or your lives! If the boat is more important, fine. But I promise that when I take you to shore, I'll build a house for your family and find jobs for you as well. What do you think? Time is running out."

Saarieun decides by himself, saying, "Okay, I agree. But while my father is alive, he won't agree to this so you must wait until he dies. Then I'll give you this boat. Do you agree?"

"Okay, but this must be a legally binding agreement," the foreign boat owner replies.

"Okay, I agree," Saarieun responds.

Then everyone on the foreign boat helps them and they become relieved.

The next day, Mr Sieun regains consciousness. Mingsaat informs him of what occurred last night without mentioning Saarieun's agreement with the foreign boat owner.

Hearing this, Mr Sieun prays to the heavens, "Thank you for saving our lives. I'll never forget that you've given us a second chance."

The foreign boat comes again and tows the family to an island. Then the boats separate and Saarieun follows the foreign boat owner's directions.

The wife of the foreign boat owner is unhappy with her husband now and asks, "Why did you show them the way?"

"I just showed them the wrong way," her husband replies. "It might be a long time until Mr Sieun dies, so I just directed them to a deserted island. They won't be able to fight us there." They laugh in amusement.

Saarieun attempts to scull the boat until he finally sees an island. "Don't take us there," Sreipou says, "because it is so far from land."

"Keep silent!" Saarieun says. "Let's follow the advice of the man who is helping us. They will assist us to find land and we can stop being fishermen. Why don't you believe them? You are so ungrateful."

Sarin mocks his brother, saying, "If they want to help us, why are they directing us to an island and not to shore?"

"They are helping us because they want our boat. You know that!" says Sreipou.

"That's what I think," Sarin says. "If I were you, I'd rather be dead than give the boat away."

"Stop talking like this," Saarieun responds.

"I must say this because I want father to hear," Sarin replies. "The foreign boat owner doesn't want to help us. They want our boat and you are selling it to them. You are making a mistake."

Saarieun, who doesn't want to listen, gets angry and strikes his brother with the scull, giving him a gash on the head and knocking him out. Then he threatens his mother and sister, saying, "This is what happens to someone who lies."

Mr Sieun becomes very troubled about this situation. He has started to understand more about Saarieun's plans. He wants to hit his son but can't because he is so weak. Tears are streaming down his face as he does nothing.

Saarieun glares at his brother and sister as they bandage his brother's head, then, glowering at his father, he cries, "Father don't be angry at me! You are old so keep quiet. I can do anything, don't worry. I'm capable; I can do it."

Mr Sieun's family arrives at the deserted island. The foreign boat owner comes to provide them with food and to get information about Mr Sieun's pending death.

Mr Sieun struggles to express his last words to his wife and children, "You must keep the boat. Don't let anyone take it. Don't insult our ancestors. You must be unified; don't quarrel with each other. If you can do this, I'll die in peace."

The sea s calm as the sun sets. The Sieun family is crying on a deserted island. Their father is dead. They have buried his corpse. Everyone is full of sorrow when the foreign boat arrives and its owner talks with Saarieun.

"What I say, I do; and you too must do what you said. All foreign nationalities follow the law. Don't worry," he says, laughing.

Mingsaat picks up a stick to attack him. "You are going to die!" she shouts. "You are a thief!" But she is weak and cannot win because they have a gun. The foreign boat owner pulls out his gun and shoots several times, ordering his workers to fight.

They break Sarin's legs as Saarieun stands by watching, but he protects his mother, saying, "Mother, I told you all ready that it is better to remain silent but you didn't believe me. There are many of them. They have guns. How can we win?"

His mother replies, "Huh! You are a bad son. Why did you agree to this? Please go away; I don't want to see you."

Saarieun and the owner of the foreign boat leave together.

This is the result of conflict: the foreign boat owner can keep Mr Saarieun's boat just like he planned. He comforts Saarieun, saying: "Since I'm a foreigner, I follow the law and keep my contract." The owner gives Saarieun the job of managing the workers on his father's old boat.

Saarieun makes them work day and night to satisfy the owner of the foreign boat. The workers labour hard but remain very poor. They are the weak people. Some are widows, others are disabled or orphans, all living on the boat without purpose.

Everything is controlled by Saarieun. All his family are living like immigrants on their former boat. The boat is being improved, its name changed to a foreign name. It looks nothing like the original. The family is sad but they can do nothing. It will never be their property again. Now everything has changed.

In the end, this family is so sad. It's never going to get better for them. Saarieun is also sad, but he has no choice because the owner of the foreign boat has all the power. He must order them to work incessantly even though they are all Khmer.

Everything is hard. Everyone will remain poor until death. They have lost their identity as one family and nationality. They've lost all the prosperity they once had.

7

"Obscure Way'' won first place in short fiction at the Nou Hach Literary Competition, 2006. It was published in Khmer with English translation in the Nou Hach Literary Journal, Vol. 3. It is a coming of age story for a young college student from the countryside attending university in the big city Phnom Penh. His exploits provide opportunity for maturation as his expectations about love and city life meet with disappointment.

Obscure Way

Pen Chhornn

At the beginning of 2006, I've started to ponder my future deeply. It is due to all the text message New Year's wishes that I receive on my phone—wishing me success, wealth, honor, and patriotic feeling—that lead me to think beyond the courses I had taken at the university. I start asking myself the following questions: How can I maintain good health? What kind of work would bring me more income? How can I gain respect? What about my patriotism?

I could never come up with satisfactory answers to the above questions. I am aware of my limitations, but I cannot stop thinking. I'll try to stop obsessing about these questions by picking a good role model and follow his way to success.

I start reading philosophy books. I have learned a little bit about the lives of philosophers in both Western and Asian countries. I read about Mahatma Gandhi, the Indian philosopher who promotes non-violence; Nicolo Machiavelli, the Italian political philosopher; Confucius, a Chinese philosopher; and the Greek philosopher Aristotle. Through reading the biographies and masterpieces of these great men, my mind slips out of Khmer society. I fully appreciate the wisdom of great men who are followed by the world's people. At the same time I feel ashamed for being so unrealistic but cannot prevent myself from thinking that way. I try switching off my mind and just allow time to pass.

Today I meet my friend. I share all my thoughts with her. She gives me a simple answer: "You don't need to pick a great man as your role model. You can simply pick a Cambodian who is prominent, holds a good position, and is wealthy, such as a medical doctor, movie star, or idol singers. . . whomever you admire, follow him. Then you will be successful."

After a brief exchange of ideas, I leave her. Pondering her comments, I realize that what she said is true and right. In Cambodia there must be honorable wealthy men. No doubt. I believe I will be able to find a role model. I try to figure out the way to discover a good person. I am certain that no books in the library have been written about these Cambodians yet.

My eagerness to strengthen myself as a better student causes my mind to wander; finally it brings me back to someone close at hand, my neighbor. This man owns a big villa surrounded by a cement wall and topped by barbed wire. At the front door, there is a sign "Beware of Dogs" and a twenty-four-hour guard.

I have often chatted with this villa's guard Uncle Sakrava. He knows that I am a student. He always chats with me about various issues: life, politics, corruption, the past and the future of the country, his own past and the international news. Sometimes, we have talked late into the night.

Today the cool, early February weather has arrived with Chinese New Year. The music of the Lion Dance beings along the street and in the house where the dancers are performing. Uncle Sakrava is not busy since the owner of the villa went to his family's native village to celebrate Chinese New Year.

Smiling, he calls to me, "Hey Teacher, aren't you going to celebrate Chinese New Year like everybody else?"

"No, Uncle," I answer through my window.

"You have light skin. Why don't you observe Chinese customs?"

I don't answer but go down to see him instead. Uncle Sakrava brings out all kinds of food—Chinese soup, Beijing duck, stir fry duck, special roast pork, chicken drunkard—puts them on a cement table and asks me to join him, "Come on Teacher; don't be shy."

"I've never had this kind of food before, such tasty dishes."

"I thought you had Chinese blood?" Uncle Sakrava is trying to pin me down.

"Not so, I'm pure Khmer. Just look at me and you should know."

"Let's eat." Uncle Sakrava pushes me to consume his food. "Forget about the bloodline. We can just pretend to be Chinese for one day. In our country, right now, people intermingle; some of our people get drunk before the Chinese New Year. Look at grandma Sao's house," he points to the house across the street. "It is quiet. She stopped selling Cambodian noodles and went out for a ceremony somewhere. I can't find anything for breakfast. Let's drink our first glass, teacher."

He lifts up his glass to toast; his glass touches mine with a clinking sound. He then picks up a piece of meat with his chopsticks, puts it in his mouth and chews with a crunchy sound. He asks, "Teacher, how about the present situation of our country? Can we become economically developed like Japan or the United States?"

I am not able to answer these questions. I haven't thought that far yet. I just came to the city a few months ago. I haven't really adjusted to city life yet or been able to understand all of these social issues.

"So, forget that," he says. "Just pay attention to your studies. As for me, I am aware of my own situation. I will never have a brilliant future. I will barely survive. The little money I make is just enough to send to my wife in the village. Look, Teacher!" He holds up his shirt for me to see a scar from a stomach wound he received as the result of fighting with the Khmer Rouge at the border. "After fighting and defending the country, I now end up as the guard of a wealthy man's house!"

He finishes his second glass of beer and adds: "What can we do? Our society is changing so rapidly."

I observe that Uncle Sakrava's face has turned red and he has become more talkative. I want to stop him from talking and escape; but I feel that it is rude to behave that way, so I am trying to be patient. I continue listening to him.

He talks about himself. "Nowadays, I feel hopeless since I have no knowledge, no skills. When I grew up, I was trained to be an electrician, and then I got into the army to serve the country. When I fought, I barely escaped death, Then, when the country was at peace, my salary was not enough to raise my children. I decided to get out of the army and take what I could for work. I tell you this story, because I see you are still young and you feel like my own child."

"Thank you, I also consider you as my parent," I answer.

"Heuw!" He takes a deep breath. "Speaking to you, I am relieved. Don't mind me much." He refills his glass and continues: "Our country has been facing difficulty for a long time. If we continue in this situation, how can our nation progress like other countries?"

"I am part of the younger generation. I don't see any difference between the past and present society in our country. Can you share with me?"

"Sure!" He gulps down half a glass of beer. "I have lived through a few regimes. The Khmer Rouge was the worst one. The other two regimes were not so good either, but at least people had enough food to eat. They had reasonable salaries, not like our present regime where teachers have to be motorcycle-taxi drivers. They do it as a side job just to survive. We are now like birds in cages. We can only read or watch the news they want us to know about in the paper or on TV."

"I don't understand you, Uncle."

"Simple. I just want to tell you that everything belongs to a different group. I can start with the newspaper. Everyday a different person is praised. You may have heard about corruption. Should such people get an opportunity, they grasp it quickly. We human beings need to survive; we wish to be rich, especially the teachers. Forgive me if I am influencing your feelings."

We both raise our glasses and cheer up. He continues talking: "Teacher, don't take me seriously. I am kind of drunk. If I make no sense, ignore it. Forgive me." He raises his hands respectfully in prayer.

I raise my palms pressed together in respectful response and assure him, saying: "Don't mention it, I don't mind."

Uncle Sakrava continues: "I speak about what I know. Don't you know? The owner of this house is a big shot trusted by many people, including myself. He is from abroad and has obtained a higher degree of education. He is patriotic, coming back to help the country by patiently trying to serve people. Until now, I have worked for him over three terms of political office. He still maintains a good reputation among politicians. It is not easy to earn such a good name. What is going on with him? I don't know much. I tell you. In our present society, you can't do anything much without money. I am sure you know that in the old times our forest timber, was simply for our own people—to build their houses and to use for firewood. It was not a disaster like it is now. Public buildings have been sold. Commune offices also have been sold to businessmen. Nephew!" He switches from calling me Teacher to Nephew. "Some of those in good positions are fortunate. I guess both of us are unlucky. You seem to have a good sense of sincerity. Let's have one more glass. If you can't, don't push yourself. You may get drunk."

"Yes, Uncle. I actually cannot drink much beer. I just want to keep you company and listen to your thoughts. I am fond of listening to you. You know much about social problems and seem to have a clear analysis."

"Don't believe much of what I say. I am speaking off the top of my head. I have never attended the university. Speaking of social problems, we all know about them and can discuss the issues equally. So far I haven't heard any of your opinions. You may belong to a certain political faction. Should I touch upon your interests, don't call the police to arrest me. I am old." He touches my shoulders lightly.

"Not at all. Don't ever think that way. I am simply a student. I just got into the university. But listening to you, I feel like I've been through five years of college. No one has ever told me this much."

"Hey! Have some fruit." He hands me a plate of fruit and then continues: "If you study at school and ignore society's problems, you won't be able to catch up with social trends."

"Thank you, Uncle, for giving me advice. It is true that

knowledge from school won't be enough to promote a better life. The owner of this villa has plenty of food. He must be nice. Is he in the political group that you mentioned?"

"Hey, Teacher. I have not included the owner of this house in what I told you." The guard is now defensive. "The corrupt people I've been talking about come from what I've heard other people say. There . . . ," he points to a man on a motorcycle, ". . . if you want to know the truth, ask him. That motorcycle-taxi driver tells me about corrupt people during his free time. He knows how much it costs to buy each government position. Teacher, you should not believe all of these rumors. You just analyze what you hear and make your own judgment."

"It's okay. If you say so, I believe you. You are such an idealist you wouldn't be working for the owner of this villa unless he was a good person."

He nods his head saying, "You are smart, Teacher . . . I am an idealist, I admit it."

Uncle Sakrava seems to be having a personal crisis. Listening to him, I can tell he is very angry with society. He hates his daily life and doesn't seem to be satisfied with what he has, even though he makes one hundred dollars a month from this job that helps to support his family in the village. He doesn't have much education, but he does have profound ideas, making it difficult to understand him.

He asks to be excused for a moment to feed his boss's dogs, German Shepherds, in the kennel. He says to the dogs, "Let's eat. If you don't, you will become skinny and your master will blame me. After eating, you should go to sleep. Don't bark. You may disturb our neighbors. While serving your master, I have to serve you, too . . ."

He throws a piece of meat to them. They fight for it, making a scary noise. He groans, "You dogs are lucky. You have become the dogs of a wealthy, big shot; you get to sleep and eat unfettered. You even have a doctor to treat you regularly. I have to collect your poop —smelly poop."

I don't much like to hear his complaints regarding the dogs' poop. When he gets back to me, I try to switch the topic, inquiring about the people who live in this villa instead.

"Uncle! Does everyone in this house have a job? How much does each of them make? How can they maintain this big house? How can each of them own a car?"

"Hum!" Uncle Sakrava clears his throat and says: "They have jobs and do other business at the same time. Don't you know? The lady of the house is doing real estate business and timber business. She owns five factories and invests in an import-export business. The man, the owner of the house, holds a high position in government. His son is on the police force. His youngest daughter is working for an NGO. All of them are capable. This is why their family is prospering."

After an additional big gulp of beer, he continues: "The lady owns 17 houses to rent, but this family does not brag about their wealth. All the children in this house hold higher degrees—a Masters or Doctorate degree. Think about that, Teacher! We can't even find a job, but they are complaining about being too busy, tired, and having no time for a vacation abroad."

I really like listening to Uncle Sakrava, but it is now getting really late. I decide to tell him that I have to go. He is reluctant to see me leave, saying: "You leave me alone? I will be bored, but I will see you later."

I say goodbye and retire.

Tonight is a pleasant evening. A soft breeze blows through my window, carrying along the sweet fragrance of Kdang Gnea flowers. Suddenly, the sound of firecrackers breaks out everywhere. The smell of gunpowder penetrates my room, reminding me of a time when the country was at war.

Time flies. I am also keeping myself busy. Everyday, I try to read books, such as novels or poems, history and philosophy. I check the Internet to dig for the information I need to research social issues as Uncle Sakrava has advised. What I read the most are articles about corruption; the poor educational system; sewing factory issues; demonstrations for equal rights and freedom of expression; salary increases, especially for teachers; poverty in remote areas; the Khmer Rouge trial; sex trafficking; border issues; and movie-star scandals. There are so many negative social issues, even monks don't get respect from the general public. As for the international news, I read about the war in the Middle East; nuclear proliferation in Iran; the bird flu; military rule in Burma; the Thai government's problem with their southern provinces; demonstrations to oust Thaksin in Thailand and Arroyo in the Philippines. Domestic and international news may cause headaches for all the leaders involved.

At this point, my thoughts sympathetically return to my villagers who live far away from the modern world. All they have to worry about is their daily lives, praying for enough rain, hoping that the goddess of rain provides mercy. All their attention is on farming. That is why they have not prospered. On the other hand, people in the city, where there is a civilized life style, are working to seek opportunities to improve their intellectual ability and to compete for a better position in life.

Some of my villagers, who have the opportunity to live abroad, still don't care much about their education. My poor villagers! When people from outside come to take away their land and sell it to someone else, no one dares to complain. If my villagers, both the docile and the cruel ones, should have a small land conflict, they provoke a life-and-death confrontation.

I've had the opportunity to come to the city to attend the university; but, I wonder, will I be able to catch up with the fortunate people whom I've just been talking about. I still have some unanswered questions in my mind: How can I earn money? How can I get a powerful position? How long should it take?

I finally realize that if I pile up all of these questions mentally, I may fall into a hopeless situation and won't be able to pursue my studies at the university. My view: life is difficult. What we wish to attain, to embrace, always slips through our fingers. It is not easy to bring our vision to actuality.

I have come to my own conclusion that effort needs to be made for whatever we may want. I am aware that my mind is unorganized. It jumps around here and there. This time, my mind switches to thinking about Corolla, a beautiful girl at the university. I haven't seen her for a while. I miss her. I love her.

Why do I love her? I can't answer that. My subconscious seems to tell me that I have fallen in love with the only girl who pays attention to me, who understands me, who knows what I'm up to.

Corolla is a generous person. She supports me when I'm

down and even supports my ambition to be knowledgeable. The books I read are the presents that she gives me. Without her, my life would be hopeless. Corolla is truly beautiful. Whenever I think of her, my love increases. Corolla's beauty, attitude, and her relationship with me make my classmates jealous. The rumor about our relationship has spread among friends. This makes me shy away, and my feelings are torn apart between her and my lessons.

While sitting by myself on a bench under the tree at the university, I am struck by the sound of a voice: "What are you thinking? I've been walking towards you and you don't even call out to me."

"I'm thinking."

"Are you thinking of me?"

"Yes, I am thinking of you and my lessons." I can hardly speak since I'm so shy about being in love with her.

"Haven't you received any money from home? Why are you less cheerful than usual and appear so weak? All right, here is 100 dollars." She hands the money to me. I am reluctant about taking her money but cannot refuse.

Corolla adds, "This is your spending money. You don't need to pay me back. Don't worry. I don't want anything from you; I'm just trying to be helpful."

"Thank you very much," I say to her.

"Look! Even the police have become thieves." She hands me the newspaper.

"Read it and you'll know," I respond. "Don't judge them. Sometimes, we don't see their side. The Greek philosopher Socrates said that no one wants to be bad. The story of police becoming thieves is widely disseminated. Everybody knows. It is a repeated story."

"I think our society won't be able to have a brilliant future," she replies. "Consider my family. At first they appear to be good. Everyday, my mom advises me to work hard on my studies and to observe closely the code of women's conduct based on Cambodian customs. Sometimes, she points out some corrupt people and asks me not to follow in their footsteps. Even you, she advises me not to associate with you, saying that you are poor. My mom has been criticized by her own children for putting other people down."

"Let it be. We should stop talking about anything that disturbs us." I cut her short as I don't want to hear anything about her family. "People these days quickly take advantage of an opportunity. We are students. We should just pay attention to our studies."

"You talk like that, but you actually think a lot about everything. I'm telling you that everyone, even you and me, can distinguish between good and bad, black and white; but many times, we are dominated by money and government influence that makes us loose our conscience. Should you like to have a long lasting relationship with me, train yourself to be a conscious person. Today you criticize others for being corrupt and support demonstrations with burning tires to protest the government. Can you assure me that you will be so pure when you get a job in the future? If not, you don't need to earn any degree from school."

I am struck by her words but decide not to respond, remembering a saying: "A man should know how to be a good loser; don't fight with a woman, and then you will succeed." I wonder why Corolla warns me so much? I try to be patient. It might ruin our friendship if I respond. I have to be careful since I'm falling in love with her. I decide to put up with her comments. She just smiles and tells me not to think so much about politics.

We decide to part. Corolla walks away and I watch as she leaves. Her way of walking is so graceful that it doubles my love for her.

I talk to myself. "Okay, Corolla. You may not know that I am thinking of you. I truly love you—love you honestly." I'm in a trance because I miss my sweetheart; I'm longing for her.

Corolla's shadow disappears, but I am still longing for her. Her smile lingers in my mind, floating deeply in my heart. Before leaving, she told me not to think about social and political issues. I sense she may be afraid that I will go crazy. I am aware myself of that possibility. When I recall her words, my mind starts thinking about social and political issues right away. I cannot restrain myself from thinking about all those issues, though I know that they are complicated.

I am a common person, a university freshman, young and weak. I find it very difficult to just think about these issues. I cannot imagine the kinds of difficulties that politicians must go through. I don't know how many times I will have to reread Machiavelli in order to understand Khmer society.

Oh my! Whenever I think about social problems, I get annoyed. Being annoyed this way probably disqualifies me from being an actor on the political scene. I'm thinking to myself. My mind is lingering and doesn't go any further. Since I've started courses at the university, my view of society is always negative.

This is the beginning of April. That means Khmer New Year is coming soon. I am bored. To get out of this condition, I withdraw my own personal savings to have some fun for once . . . !

I go to a discothèque. Chenda, a girl who works at the bar, comes to join my table, making me feel happy. The bar is full of smoke making it difficult for me to breathe. Most of the girls who work here are wearing sexy dresses. People at this place don't dance Khmer style. They do Western dances such as Bolero, Cha-Cha, Rock, and slow dance. They don't dance properly. They simply hug each other. Old people are fondly hugging the young girls. Chenda tells me that she doesn't know how to dance. She says she is working in this bar only for money.

Oh my! I'm looking for fun, but running into a tragic situation. In this bar I am thinking a lot about the fate of the Cambodian girls who work here, being belittled by rich men. They, in fact, have no fun. Some nostalgic old songs make those dancers enjoy hugging each other.

I can't stand it any longer and decide to go home. On my way back, I see a big casino. I feel a little eager to explore what might be happening inside so I swing by.

Lord Buddha! The building's fancy exterior is ostentatious. Inside, people are collecting money from addicted gamblers. I happen to see Uncle Sakrava's boss in this place. He also comes here I talk to his chauffer, and he tells me that his boss comes here to do money laundering. I don't understand this term and never had any sense of its illegality. I never want to observe illegal actions but always seem to encounter them. This is what I have come to think.

I leave the casino and continue my meandering trip back home. I am struck by some colorful lights sparkling in front of me. Out of curiosity, I swing by the place. I see the sign "Karaoke, Fair

Price." Now I feel like trying out my voice. I see many beautiful girls in a big room who call me "handsome man."

"Hey! Handsome man, what kind of song do you want to sing?"

"Pagoda Kids," I request.

"We don't have any tragic songs, handsome man. Try a different one—a modern song."

"What's a good modern song that you have?" I ask.

"There are plenty of Preap Sovat and Midada's songs. Pick one."

"Hmm, I'd like you to play 'Little Hope,' a Sin Sisamut song. Do you have it?"

"Yes, still an old one, but I will play it for you."

While singing "Little Hope," Corolla's image appears in my mind. I feel I would be happy if Corolla were singing with me.

"You, handsome man, are a good singer. If you want, I'll join you. I am more than happy to do so." A young girl has made this comment.

"Why do you call me handsome man?" I ask.

A girl named Aleap smiles and answers: "Because you are handsome. This is the first night that I've had a chance to sit by a decent young man like you since I started working here. The majority of our costumers are old and because of that inappropriate. They come here not to sing but to hug the young girls. Their hands are always busy, touching here and there."

"If you disagree, how can they hug you?"

"I need money. So I just let it go."

One other girl adds, "I wasn't afraid of losing my job the other day. I gave one Ph.D. a black eye."

"Ala, you are so nasty," Aleap somewhat blames her friend.

"Ala, I've heard they don't allow people to open Karaoke shops. Why do they let you do it here?" I ask.

"Brother. Some just say; some just do. Some Karaoke shops are open just for high-class customers. How can they close such a fun place?"

I admire Ala, who does not have any education but understands political issues. Should she have an education, she would be the best human resource for the country.

I sing and think about Ala and Aleap's future. Should the song be sadder, I might cry for her. I haven't sated my pleasure yet, but it's already midnight. I say goodbye to Ala and Aleap.

"Handsome man, be careful on your way back. This late at night, you may run into a thief or get into a traffic accident. Do you hear me? Don't forget to come back. Don't forget me." Ala reminds me.

I don't really take Ala's words seriously as I feel the city is not that chaotic. I do not reply and take off on my motorcycle. I ride along singing as my mind is still on Karaoke. A car just ahead of me runs a red light and almost hits me. It frightens me. The car turns around and heads toward me making a sound like the street is being torn apart.

The driver opens the car window and yells, "Do you want to die? Didn't you see my car?"

I try not to talk back, but I wonder, "Why am I at fault? The green light was clear to me."

The driver continues, "Your life is cheaper than my car. Next time, be careful or else you'll die."

I feel astonished at hearing this. It's beyond my comprehension.

Now it's dawn. Why don't I hear the bread vendor's voice as I usually do every morning? I wake up feeling tight. I have a headache and can't even raise my hands. Where am I? What is wrong with me?

Then I realize that I'm in the hospital. True! I remember that last night I was hit from behind. Oy! I am in so much pain. I recall now. Had I taken Ala's advice seriously, I might not have run into this accident. I learn that my story is in the newspaper. I am so ashamed. I try to console myself by blaming society, thinking that if everyone had a good education, our society would be orderly with no thieves or car accidents.

Corolla visits me in the hospital. I tell her the whole story of what happened to me last night. She blames me for being involved in such crazy acts. She says that I should not have gone to a bar, Karaoke place or casino at all. I somewhat agree with her, but try to reason that they create those places for fun. That makes her very angry. I ask her, "What can I do? Is there any harmless fun?"

"You are stupid," she says and walks away.

I am out of the hospital and happy to see Uncle Sakrava. He tells me he knew I'd been robbed, according to the newspaper he'd read. He doesn't blame me, but advises me saying, "Learn by doing, be thoughtful. For what happened to you, consider yourself lucky. You have survived, un-crippled."

"You are right. If I'd died, my parents in the village would be disappointed," I answer.

"Oh, Teacher. Do you plan to go home?"

"No, I've decided not to go. I need to look for a job. I went out for just one night but lost so much money, along with my motorcycle and cell phone."

Uncle Sakrava asks me to substitute for him as the guard at the villa. He wants to visit his wife and children since he hasn't gone home for years. I agree to take his place, to at least make some money to sustain my studies.

Life as a guard is not easy. I cannot sleep peacefully since I'm so busy opening the gate as soon as the owner of the house honks his car horn. I have to feed the dogs, to sweep the front porch, to wash the car and mow the lawn. This first work experience has almost burnt me out.

This evening his Excellency, the owner of the house, has organized a New Year's party. Most guests are big shots who drive very expensive cars. Their wives wear diamonds to show off and frequently call each other "in-law." Those big shots raise their glasses and toast each other happily.

"Best wishes for the New Year," says the owner of the house.

The sound of clinking glasses continues as part of the good cheer. I hear everyone share his or her story. They speak openly about which jobs make good money and which positions are open due to the removal of some high-ranking government official.

The party is over. The lady of the house asks her husband: "Why did you invite Mr A to the party? He does not get along well with you."

"You don't understand. Politicians don't only associate with friends. I actually didn't want to invite him, but he is very close to the big boss. Whatever he says, the big boss agrees to. The other day, he proposed that Mr C, who quit our group, replace Mr B and the boss did that."

"You are a profound thinker," the lady of the house says.

"I'd really like to change my work for a job with better money, but it costs too much. I should wait for the next election since this term is almost over. Heu! Political business requires big capital," her husband explains.

"Honey! Help our children get official government positions. They've been back from studying abroad long enough."

"Allow them to save money, and then we can think about that. It won't be too late. Don't worry about them. They've obtained a Ph.D.; not bad."

I admire rich men, big shots. Each day, they try to figure out how to get a good position and how to make more money; though they have to bite the others. This reminds me of what one wise man said: "Human beings are like wolves."

As for me, I had renounced most of my pleasurable activities through the whole New Year by working as a guard. I actually made less money than I'd spent for that one night at the bar, Karaoke place, and casino.

Uncle Sakrava returns with a sad face. He tells me that he is going to quit his job. He has asked for his last wages and will return to the village. He also tells me the sad story about his land being stolen by a powerful businessman and his two sons becoming gangsters in the village. He says that he had no fun while he was at home, using all his savings to pay off debts, and that he has received no military pension for two months.

Before we part, Uncle Sakrava advises me to study diligently He tells me that I should visit him at his village if I have time. I admit to him that I cannot help much in this situation. I have a deep sympathy for him. I decide to share part of the money I've earned from working as a guard and give it to him so he can use it as travel expenses for his return home. We part sadly.

The effects of the New Year still linger on. Students have gone back to school. I come to the university with a sense of unease.

I meet my classmates. They all talk about how much fun they had during the New Year break.

Some of my friends suspect that I must have had a lot of fun with Corolla. Some notice that I am pale. They say that I may have done something strange. They tease me. Then laughter breaks out as Corolla approaches. She stares at them and turns to greet me.

"How are your mom and dad? Have you gone to the village?"

"I don't know about my parents because I wasn't able to return home. I was busy with studies," I told her softly, just a short, unclear answer.

"Huh! Why were you studying during vacation?"

"I . . . I was working as a guard. I didn't go home." I told her honestly.

"If you were that desperate, why didn't you call me? You turned your phone off. I tried to call you many times, but couldn't get through."

"How could I turn my phone on if it was stolen," I thought to myself without answering her.

I question her, "Anything else you want to ask me?" I am really upset. I don't feel like talking to anybody.

"Since you worked as a guard, you appear to be stronger than before."

"Don't be sarcastic," I say as we walk out of class. "I want to tell you . . ." I want to tell her that I love her, but I become tongue-tied since I'm afraid that she will be mad at me. Then, I change the subject. "I'm concerned that I won't be able to find a job after graduation."

"You may not find a job right away; but if you really want one, you should begin right now. You might start doing volunteer work to get some experience. There will be plenty of opportunities waiting for you. Like my fiancé, now he is the president of an import-export company. When he was a student, he volunteered for a long time without pay."

"Lord Buddha! She has a fiancé!" I thought stunned. I try to hide my feelings of love for her. I remain silent and expressionless. Corolla is a loving girl. I admire her fiancé for being so fortunate. It must be true love. It is justifiable that I shouldn't have the opportunity to live with her, because I have no solid ground, even my mind is not so organized. I actually should thank her for giving me advice I have a gut feeling that I should seriously continue my studies. Corolla's views, the ones she has shared with me, have been useful.

"Oh dear, when did you get engaged?" I ask her feeling hurt.

"During New Year. I called you, but couldn't get through." While we are talking, her fiancé comes to pick her up. Corolla speaks softly to me, "I have to say goodbye to you, Mr. Smart."

I raise my hand to wave goodbye, feeling nostalgic. She is the one who has taught me to love. I regret losing her, but I tell myself to be strong by believing that I will find another true love in my life. I should not be discouraged.

I've been living in the city and studying at the university for a while now. I have gained some knowledge of love, student life, and the truth about Khmer society. I view that society as being in darkness in the obscurity caused by a small group of people who are rich and hold high positions in government. I hardly see this group try to improve people's quality of life by creating jobs for them. Instead, they allow people to cross the border to a neighboring country to look for work. I observe clearly that the fortunate leaders are concerned only with their family and relatives to make sure that they are well off. To secure their position, they intimidate weak and poor people by creating unusual events or by scaring them. I believe everyone knows that leaders on the scene do things opposite to what they say.

I wish that, somehow, our leaders could have the same kind of experiences I've had. Then they would be able to shed light on life for ordinary people, including myself, as we try to build a future in the midst of an obscure way.

8

"The Revolver" won second place in short fiction at the Nou Hach Literary Competition, 2006. It was published in both Khmer and English in the Nou Hach Literary Journal, Vol. 3. Like "Obscure Way" it is a coming of age story, but from the perspective of a more mature individual seeking the real Cambodia after living in France since childhood.

The Revolver

Phin Santel

Author's Note:

The original story "Katouch" was written in Khmer. It was limited to twenty-five pages and I was advised not to write about the subject of love. It was also the first time I had written a story so I wasn't really sure what to write about. I wrote a story longer than twenty-five pages so the one I sent to the Nou Hach Literary Competition was a shorter version. It actually won the second-place prize for short fiction, making me a little nervous. "The Revolver" comes closer than the original story to what I have been facing from the first day that I started to write about my country. It's more about me and my difficulties than the real story itself. The real story is about a rural woman and her rice field, a water pump and a revolver.

Forget about me . . . follow the woman. I hope that you will like her as much as I do.

The fact that you came back to Cambodia didn't surprise anybody much. They already knew, since you decided to begin your studies of Khmer literature in Paris, that one day for sure you would return to Cambodia.

You ask your parents' permission since you won't be able to help them in the restaurant anymore. Smey and Deth, your youngest sister and brother, have promised they will replace you.

Except Caroline, you don't know how you can say goodbye to her. Having gone through all these years together, it is impossible to imagine how much you will be lost without her.

"Are you leaving now?" she asks in front of the boarding gate at Charles De Gaulle Airport.

"Yes," you answer spontaneously.

"Without me?" she asks.

"Because you can't go!" you say.

"How do you know I cannot go? You didn't ask me yet?" she insists.

"Because I know the answer," you reply.

Don't cry, Caroline. You cried already once when you were born. You are not going to cry again and again for your whole life. You might cry again when you die but not this time. At least not in front of me . . .

"Write to me when you arrive in Cambodia?" she requests after releasing you from her arms.

"I think it is better if we forget each other," you tell her instead of answering her question.

"Do you think so?"

"Yes."

You turn your back and leave. You let her cry in your mother's arms.

It is not true. You will never forgot her. How could you forget someone you'd made love to a thousand times? But Paris is too cold. It is difficult to live alone. She will have a lot of chances to find someone else. It is sad to live with such promises. With time, these promises would be forgotten and betrayed. Time passes, nothing remains the same. Eternity is nothing but a lie. We should not believe in eternity. Sometimes saying goodbye to someone doesn't always mean goodbye. Caroline will understand this one day.

You are very curious to know the true Cambodia. You have been watching Cambodia from far away, in every detail through all its history and literature. You believe it is not enough to know a country from reading the newspapers or listening to the radio or watching television. A lot of things remain hidden. It is for this reason that you left Paris.

You have already informed Vincent who is currently in Cambodia. Vincent is an old friend. Your parents escaped to France in 1975 because of his father Monsieur Nicolae's help. Monsieur Nicolae and your father worked together at the French Embassy before the war began. The two families remained emotionally close since then.

Vincent picks you up at the airport as you wished. You are very exhausted, due to fifteen hours on the plane and six hours of time difference between Paris and Phnom Penh. Vincent brings you to his own apartment on Sisowath Quay.

You wake up late the next morning. Suddenly you feel the heat of the sun. It is something you have been dreaming about for the last twenty years. You hurry to get out of bed. You step out on the balcony to bask in the sunshine. You cannot express how excited you are to be back again in your own country.

Vincent has been living in Cambodia for four years. His mission for the French Embassy is finished but he doesn't want to return to France. He, after all, has fallen in love with a Cambodian woman. This does not surprise you because you know your friend very well. Vincent has a great deal of knowledge about Khmer culture. He, at the moment, works at the French Cultural Center in Phnom Penh.

They get married three months later, after you arrived in Cambodia. They celebrate with a traditional Khmer wedding. Thyda, his wife, is very beautiful. She has dark shiny skin. She looks like a little girl but not quite as small. You find her very cute. The two of them seem made for each other. Your parents and Vincent's parents fly a long way from Paris to Phnom Penh to join his wedding. Your father wants to introduce you to some good daughters of his old friends. But you tell him you are just twenty-five years old, too young to get married. You want to remain like a wild man for some more time.

A few days after the wedding, Vincent and Thyda go to Europe for their honeymoon. They let you live alone in their apartment on Sisowath Quay. Your parents also go back to France because they are concerned about their restaurant. You have to live alone with your solitude. It is said that solitude is good for a writer. He can imagine so many things from solitude. But for you nothing goes well. You have been in Phnom Penh for three months; still you have nothing seriously to write about.

You dream of being able to write a love story about Cambodia. You were ashamed when you searched all the world's libraries but could find only books on Cambodia about genocide, stories of blood and survival. You want the world to find a different book about Cambodia. You came here for this reason. You came to this country to write a book.

"What kind of book are you writing?" asks a woman one day.

"A love story," you reply.

"A love story? What kind of love story? Do you think that love exists in this country?"

"Yes, love exists in the heart of every human being. Wherever a person exists, there is a heart. And when there is a heart, there is love. Isn't this enough for you to believe love exists in Cambodia?" You question her in return.

"Can I read your story?"

"I haven't written it yet. I don't know what kind of love story to write . . . ".

What kind of love story can you write? Every day, for three months, you find only accident reports and police reports about murders and crimes. The country is still suffering from poverty. People need to survive. They don't have time to think about love or any other emotional engagement. There are only a few teenagers and other people who can close their eyes and remain ignorant of all the depressing events occurring in society.

It is said that Cambodia provides what you want. You can make love with all kinds of women. You can invite the beer girls or Karaoke girls for "night soup," a secret code of invitation if you don't dare ask a girl directly for sex. You can also have a waitress from a restaurant in your bed if you have the right contacts. You can even ask a high school student or a market vendor to your room if you have the right contacts. You could also have a singer or movie star illuminate your night if you have the right contacts. It depends on how much you have in your pocket. This country is crazy about money.

You try to escape and avoid all these things. It is hard, after all, to imagine something else. The surrounding environment makes you feel completely lost. When you get lost, only women can say who you are and what to do. Women are the mothers of everything. A woman can give you thousands of reasons to live, especially when she moves her hands and caresses your hair. A woman can make you feel alive or make you angry. You don't wait for the big thing from her. You just wait until she puts her finger in her mouth. It was very simple. Without women, you are hopeless. You are zero. You find nothing to write about in this country; but from women's naked bodies, you find thousands of mysteries to discover. At least you can find a story from every woman that you make love with.

You begin to show up frequently at the bars downtown, especially the Heart of Darkness, a very small, pleasant bar at the corner of Pasteur Street.

"Would you like to buy me a drink?" A young, lovely woman asks one evening.

"Sorry? What did you just say?" You ask in surprise.

You don't believe what you've just heard. It is rare to hear a real Cambodian woman ask a guy to buy her a drink. She doesn't even look like any of the prostitutes that you know here.

"Buy me a drink!" She repeats.

"OK." You order a whisky for her.

"Is this seat taken?"

"Hmm . . . Not really. . . it could be yours if you'd like to sit down."

"Oh, I see. Would you like to dance?"

"With you?"

"Yes with me, would you like to dance with me?"

How can you refuse a pretty woman's request? She comes from nowhere and appears in front of you like an angel. She treats you like someone she has known for a hundred years. You feel very passionate about making love to her. She is like a starving wild animal, gone without food for three months.

However, there is something she doesn't tell you. She doesn't tell you that she is the mistress of a Taiwanese gangster. She doesn't tell you that she goes out at night to get vengeance on her man. It is because he has abandoned her for one week to visit his wife in Taiwan. She is sad and has an emergency need. You never think that she would be able to endanger you. It is as people say: "Women are dangerous and the most beautiful women are the most dangerous."

It starts from there, in the Heart Darkness, that you get to know Sam. He lets you live. If it had not been for him, you probably would have been killed without being able to say a single word. It is not good to deceive a woman who belongs to someone else. A woman, whether here or there, cannot be shared. If you want to try, you will be killed in silence.

This is the evening the gangster returns to see his mistress. This woman, she does not love you at all, or at least she is not willing to protect you. She leaves with her master without saying anything. You never believed that this woman could leave you without a single word. Sam receives his boss's order to eliminate you from this world. He takes you to a place far from the city. He waits for the right moment to shoot you with his revolver. You already believe that you are going to die without being able to say anything. But we die only once; why not resist, at least with words before the end?

"I cannot die!!!" You shout with all your strength.

"Why? Why can't you die? You are playing around with someone else's woman. You must die. Isn't it justifiable, no?" Sam asks you with a smile.

"It's because I haven't done what I want to do yet."

"What do you want to do, precisely?"

"Write a story!!!"

"What kind of story do you think you can write about this country?" He asks you.

"A love story."

"Love story? What kind of love story? Do you think that love exists in this country? Do you believe that deceiving someone else's woman is a love story? Is that what you think?"

"No, no . . . It was a mistake. I made a mistake. It is true that I am going to die. To die today or tomorrow is nothing important.

But before I die, I want to at least finish writing one story."

"Do you believe that you actually can finish one?"

"I've already got some ideas."

"When can I read it?"

"If you kill me now, how can I write it?"

You don't know if Sam can wait to read your love story. You don't know if you will or will not be able to finish this story one day. The important thing is that he doesn't kill you. He lets you live. This good man later becomes a very sincere friend. He has worked for the Taiwanese gangster for a few months. You ask him why he chooses this job. He tells you that he doesn't have a choice. He has a lot of debt to pay after having lost so many soccer bets. The boss has lent him a sum of money to pay them off.

It is also for this reason that his wife Sim comes to look for him. He hasn't sent money or any news back home for the past three months. His wife has been worried about him. Sam and Sim grew up together in the same family. Sam was an orphan. His parents were killed during the Khmer Rouge regime. Sim's family found Sam on the street while they were returning to the village after 1979. Sam has lived with Sim's family since then.

Sam can do everything an ordinary man can usually do. He is a serious man. It is because of his qualities that Sim's family married him to their daughter when he reached twenty. Sim, with the arrangement from her parents and also with her will, got married so young. She was only eighteen. She didn't know anything about love. She didn't know what she should do after getting married. Sam could not get close to Sim for the first three months. Sam fell from the bed every night after trying to get close to his wife. You don't know how Sam could make love to his wife. You don't know what he did so that Sim finally agreed to make love. You have heard it said how this happens to some rural women. It's because they don't know anything about love.

Sim knows how to grow rice. She knows how to raise cows. She knows how to clean the house. She knows how to cook. Moreover she's good at it. She wakes up early in the morning at four a.m. to cook. She knows how to make other things. But there are some things she doesn't know. She doesn't know why she's been sad since her husband left her to work in the city, since he hasn't returned home. She doesn't even realize that she is sad.

"Do you love him, your husband?"

"I don't know . . . I don't know what to say. I don't know about love . . . I don't know how to talk about it . . . how to love . . ."

"But why do you come look for him?"

"I worry about him."

"So then, that means you think about him a little I imagine?"

"Yes, I think about him all the time, all night long. I want him to come back home. I want him close to me to help grow rice, to raise cows, and to do other work."

"But it doesn't have anything to do with your wanting to kiss him, for example? Rather to reassure yourself that he still loves you? Or to tell you his feelings in sweet words of love?"

"I don't know about any of that. He never spoke to me of love. Nor I...I don't know how to say big things. I don't know. . . "

"I see that you love him a lot, this man. I can see it in you, this love. Why can't you feel anything? It exists in you, I'm certain of it."

"I don't know. I want him back home with me. I also need a water pump."

"Why is a pump necessary?"

"It's because there's not enough rain, not enough water in the rice field. We need a machine to pump water. Otherwise, the rice will die."

Sam leaves home because the rice paddy doesn't yield enough rice to support his family. He starts working in the city two years ago, in a car garage. He sends all the money he earns to his wife every month. He is a great man. It is his mistake betting on soccer matches. You believe he did it to return home with a bit of money in his pocket. He doesn't know that soccer is just a great choice for loosing all his money.

There are a lot of people in this country and many who are obsessed with games. They are poor and would like to have a little more money.

Sam leaves his wife with you without telling you what he is up to or where he is going. You only know that he has a very important task to finish tonight. He says it will be his last job, his last payback from his boss. If he is successful, he will be returning to the countryside with his wife.

After her husband leaves, Sim cannot remain calm. Her concern becomes more and more intense. She is afraid that something unfortunate will happen to her husband. She walks from right to left, from left to right. She descends and ascends the stairs many times. She comes to you asking the same questions: "Where is he now? What's taking him so long?"

You don't know how to help this woman. You don't want her crying either. Suddenly you think of a place you hope may calm her down. You bring her to Dangkal Temple, a place where people usually pray for happiness and blessings for those they love.

Sim does this. She prays for Sam. It is said that the Dangkal deity is a good lord. Whatever people ask for comes true because of the power of the Dangkal god. You don't believe in gods; but when you see Sim pray, you pray for her. You hope that Sam will return safely and in good health. Then he can take his wife back to the countryside.

After prayers are done, you take her to the old market to buy groceries so she can prepare a meal. You don't know what to do to make her happy. You think that cooking will reduce her anxiety about her husband. In the kitchen, you try asking many questions to keep her occupied. You find out this woman doesn't know how to speak her mind. She is very shy. Every time you ask her a question, her face turns red. She is very shy when speaking about love. You find out a lot of funny things, especially when she tells you about pushing her husband off the bed every night when he first tried to touch her. This way you learn a lot about their time together early in their marriage.

But you cannot fool her for long with conversation . . .

After the meal, she is doing nothing but walking around, going to watch the people down along Sisowath Quay. She goes up and down the stairs looking for Sam multiple times. Her husband is not back yet. You drive her in the car Vincent left for you. You tour the city to calm her down a little. She is looking for her husband on every street. She doesn't get bored looking at every street corner, looking for her husband. She doesn't stop even one minute to rest. You can see it in her eyes, the deep worry she has for her husband.

You bring her to the Heart of Darkness, the place where you first met Sam. But he is not there.

Where is he?

It is a question you cannot answer. At two a.m. you finally manage to get Sim back home. She is tired but doesn't want to go to bed. She is sleeping in the front room waiting to open the door for her returning husband. You don't want to sleep either. You want to write something about this woman. She touches you deeply, with her silence, her unspeakable feelings she doesn't know how to express. She keeps everything inside. If you were her, at least you would be able to say something. But she doesn't know how to communicate feelings.

But what could we speak about, love?

Hours pass; you find no words either. Can this woman's feelings be expressed in words? Do we have some words to exchange that could relieve her concern?

It is too hard, you find, for her to keep everything suppressed. You keep searching for the exact words until someone knocks on the door. Sim wakes up and goes before you to open it. There is Sam, finally. There he is at the door, smiling. Thank god he is still alive. Moreover he is grinning. His smile is enough to assure you that his task has been successful. Sim hugs her husband tightly.

She tells Sam repeatedly: "Don't leave me alone anymore . . . don't leave me alone anymore."

Sam wants to leave immediately, to take a taxi and head back to the countryside. You tell him to wait a moment. Then, you go get some money from your room. You give him 200 dollars. He refuses at first. You knew he would so you tell him that you are going to write a story about his wife. It is the price you will pay for her information. You believe that 200 dollars will be enough to buy a water pump for the rice field. In return Sam gives you his revolver. You don't want the gun; but if you refuse, he will not accept your money.

"What kind of story are you writing about me?" Sim asks before they leave.

"A love story."

"A love story? What kind of love story? Do you think that

you can write a love story about me?"

"Yes, love exists in everyone's heart. Wherever there is a human being, there is a heart. And with a heart, there is love. Is this not enough to make you believe there is also love in you?"

"Can I read your story?"

"I wrote it yesterday. I must reread it and correct some mistakes. I am going to bring it with me when I visit you in the countryside."

"Don't forget then to bring it with you. I want to read . . . " Sim requests very sincerely.

The next morning you go for a cup of coffee as usual in the restaurant down along Sisowath Quay. You find out by chance just glancing at the front page of a newspaper. It reads "Chinese Man Murdered Last Night". He was shot three times with a revolver. It reminds you of something. You check the bullets still in the revolver that Sam gave you. There are exactly three left.

9

Mey Son Sotheary lives and works in Phnom Penh. This short story was first published in the popular daily newspaper Reasmey Kampuchea. Her interest in women's social problems is reflected in "My Sister." It is also another coming of age story with the theme of transitioning from a rural to urban lifestyle. This story was first published in Virtual Lotus: Modern Fiction of Southeast Asia, translation by Tomoko Okada, Vuth Reth, and Teri Yamada.

My Sister

Mey Son Sotheary

It was already 7 pm. We'd been strolling happily along the boulevards of Phnom Penh, my younger sister Moum and I, oblivious to time. Nightlife in the big city especially intrigued me. Modern cars were parked around big restaurants frequented by fashionably dressed customers. We were overwhelmed by it all.

I must confess that I'm from the countryside. My village is in Prey Veng province. When my parents were alive, my dad worked for the provincial office of cultural affairs and my mother was a respected seamstress. Due to their efforts, we three children had an easy life. When my elder sister Keo finished high school, a relative took her to continue her studies in Phnom Penh.

In Prey Veng, my younger sister Moum and I had just finished junior high school when our parents died. We would have to quit school without their financial support. Fortunately, Keo insisted on our education and gave us money for school whenever she came to visit. Personally, I was delighted with the chance to continue my studies.

Keo often told us about her Phnom Penh job working for a

foreign investment firm. With such a good job she could finance our high-school education, so I felt motivated and never neglected my schoolwork. My dream was to graduate from high school, then to continue my education at any university in Phnom Penh. Finally, I passed the entrance exam for the Literature Faculty at the Royal University of Phnom Penh and Moum passed the exam for the Faculty of Law, thus fulfilling her own dream.

We moved to our relatives' home in Phnom Penh to prepare for the new school year at the university. Keo explained why she couldn't live there. She was very busy with company business, working long hours on site, so she stayed in company housing. After all, she explained, our relatives' house wasn't near her company. If she stayed with us, she would waste a lot of time commuting.

Keo only came to visit us on the weekends. I remember how the three of us were so happy then. She'd become a big city girl, the way she talked and acted. What I completely adored about her was the financial support. She made our lives so easy.

It was still exciting to stroll along the streets of Phnom Penh at night. One evening, Moum and I were out fairly late when I remembered I'd better take her back home. I worried about our stepmother, who would probably be waiting up for us. I called to my younger sister and we walked toward my motorcycle parked nearby. It was a gift from Keo so we would have some transportation to school. Just as I approached it, I noticed a group of bargirls across the street. Wearing heavy makeup, those ladies of the night were arriving and departing on motorbike-taxis in front of a bar, laughing and teasing each other. I turned to look at Moum. She was frowning at those girls.

I said, "Moum. Don't look at them!"

She glanced away. Later on the motorcycle, she asked: "San! Why are there so many girls like that in Phnom Penh?"

I knew that Moum wanted to talk about those prostitutes.

"It's the city. You'd better ignore it. It's like that in the city . . ."

Moum was silent. When we arrived home, I went to bed exhausted yet obsessed with the image of those bargirls. It's right, what Moum said, that kind of girl creates a bad impression, one that slowly destroys Cambodian values and tradition. I don't understand them. What I do know is that kind of business is a big mistake for Cambodian girls. Even if they say it's for survival, that kind of work is still completely wrong. They could clean floors, or wash noodle dishes, or sell vegetables. They could survive that way too. But that's my idea; those girls don't think like me. Anyway, I'd better forget it and get some sleep. I need my energy to study so I won't disappoint Keo, who was still working so hard to support me.

A whole year passed before I found out about it.

By then I'd grown used to city life. I'd been studying foreign languages at a private school where I did well. This encouraged me to study even harder in anticipation that after graduation I could work for a foreign company. That would enable me to financially help Keo. She still provided everything, so I never worried about the money required for my education, and my academic performance continued to improve.

Soon my fluency in several foreign languages enabled me to get a job in radio broadcasting. I translated foreign news and received quite a good salary for it. I was very happy and satisfied with this job although it meant I wouldn't finish my university studies. This job gave me hope that I would be able to support myself in the future. Now I could use part of my salary to help Keo pay for Moum's education.

It was the last night of the month when I found out. We had just been paid. Some of my friends and I went to a party at a restaurant. We had a grand time there until about 9 pm, when we decided to go home. I walked along with one of my friends who had become quite drunk.

I chided him, "Hey, come on! All of us are fine except you!"

While my friends were getting their vehicles, I walked him over to mine. My drunken friend murmured, "Hey, San, look at that girl! She's really neat! Too bad she's already in somebody else's car. I'd pay anything for her!"

I was really disgusted with his nonsense, such inconsiderate talk about those ladies of the night. I laughed uncomfortably and looked at the girl he'd admired as she got into a car across the street. I chided him again.

"Such a guy, aren't you! Whenever you get drunk, you say

anything. Let me take you home."

My friend kept mumbling, "San! She's so beautiful. Wow!"

I was really bored with him now. Since I had to steady him as he walked ahead, I just glanced at the bargirl. I was stunned when she turned her face toward me. Why did she look like my sister?

I immediately dropped my friend and rushed across the street through a path of oncoming vehicles. When I got there, I noticed she had turned to look at me in astonishment. I was shocked, feeling I'd received a death sentence. It was my sister, definitely my sister. I stood silently under her sad gaze. Then I saw two men pulling her hand so she'd get into their car. They drove off, leaving me standing there alone. I couldn't even cry.

I went back home in grief. I felt both betrayed and terribly insulted. My stepmother was watching TV in the living room when I arrived. I didn't speak to her but went directly to my room. I passed Moum's room, where she was writing something. This distressed me even more and then I noticed she was wearing the necklace Keo had just given her last week. I pondered whether to tell Moum what I'd seen when she noticed me and stopped writing.

"San! Why so late? Did you have dinner yet?"

I tried to remain calm. The truth would devastate her. I entered my room, slammed the door and took off my shirt, throwing it on the bed. I just wanted to take a shower and to forget everything I'd previously seen. But that horrible scene appeared every time I closed my eyes. Why my sister? Why had she chosen such a stupid path? Turning, I noticed the computer she'd purchased for my studies. I knocked it off the desk in rage. It broke with a loud crash on the floor. I was obsessed with the scene of my sister being pulled into some car. I kicked the computer hard so it rolled across the tile floor.

My stepfather, stepmother, and sister opened the door to my room. They looked at me with amazement. I sat down on the bed, tears streaming down my face like a little child. Moum noticed and approached me.

"San! What's the matter with you? What's wrong, San?" She asked in a choked voice.

I wanted to answer but didn't know what to say. Crying, I shook my head childishly. This was the worst moment of my entire life. I felt so hurt. I didn't understand how my sister could let herself be so degraded like that.

Having spent a sleepless night, the next morning I went to the living room exhausted. I sat down on the sofa and started to read the newspaper. Then Moum appeared.

"Aren't you going to work?"

"No," I murmured.

Next I heard Moum's happy voice as the front door opened.

"Keo! Don't you work today?"

I knew Keo would come. I suddenly blew up when I heard her quietly say: "Moum, here's some food. Eat, then go to school!"

I got up from the sofa and saw the food from Keo in Moum's hand. I rushed to grab it, then hurled the snacks on the floor, shouting: "Stop bringing that filthy stuff!"

Moum looked at me incredulously. I glanced at Keo's disheartened face as she stood in the doorway. She pushed the door closed, not wanting anyone outside the house to hear.

"Look at you!" I said. "How cheap you are. What a role model for our younger sister!" I was suffering and out of control. Right or wrong had no meaning. I just had to scold her. But suddenly Moum cut me short.

"San! Don't do that to Keo."

I looked at Moum and told her to shut up: "From now you don't take anything from her, understand? If you need something, tell me. Stop using her indecent money. You hear me?"

I saw her hesitate. Keo looked down and started to gather the snacks scattered around the floor. Moum sat down to help her. I pulled her hand, shouting, "Go to school, now!"

Moum jerked free of my grasp and stormed away, shouting: "Don't be so unreasonable! What about your rudeness to Keo?"

Frowning, I retorted: "So go ahead. Ask her what kind of work she does."

Moum answered bravely, "Whatever she does, she's still our sister. You've no right to despise her!"

I was so mad. I turned and pointed at Keo, who was still gathering the scattered food.

"Say it! Say it now! Tell her what you've been doing. Are you good enough to be our sister?"

Moum yelled at me: "San! Be careful. If you keep this up, I'll tell step mom and step dad when they get home from work. Don't be so unreasonable!"

I was still angry. Then Keo slowly stood up and carefully articulated each word: "All right. I'll tell you if you want me to."

I turned away when I heard her sobbing.

"I am an indecent bargirl. Not only that, I sell my body. I have sex with anyone who pays me well."

Before Keo finished speaking, Moum was leaning against the wall, her eyes wide with astonishment. I knew this would be devastating.

Keo continued speaking: "I know how much this hurts you. But both of you should realise I'm the one who hurts the most. Brother works for a famous company and younger sister studies law with a bright future ahead of her. But I understand. From now on don't regard me as your sister. Even if by chance we meet along the road somewhere, let's pretend not to know each other. Okay? I'll just discard these snacks. From now on, I won't dare buy anything for you since I've lost the right to be your sister."

I was looking at the plastic bag full of snacks Keo had just thrown into the trash. She turned and left. I forced back my tears since I didn't want to cry while Moum was sobbing.

Night arrived. I was sitting at a bar drinking beer when a prostitute approached me. Seeing her delighted smile, I told her to sit down, gave her ten dollars and decided to ask some questions.

"Can I ask you something?"

She laughed and answered: "I'm sitting here for you to ask, darling. For ten dollars you can ask a lot."

I was clueless about her values. Feeling awful, I asked her: "Why do you do this kind of work?"

She laughed cynically while waving the ten-dollar bill. I understood so I asked the next question.

"For money, huh? Is this the only way you can get money? With so many decent jobs available, why not find one?"

She blushed and then forced a smile.

"I'm not educated; I have no skills. What can I do? Even if I found another job, the most I could make is thirty or forty dollars a month."

I felt irritated and thought of Keo. I asked her again: "Why do you need so much money? It's true you'll earn just a small salary with an unskilled job, but it's enough for one person to survive."

Now she seemed angry and answered rudely: "Right. I can survive, just me by myself. What about you? Do you survive just for yourself and that's it? I have brothers and sisters, and they have to go to school. How can I pay for their education? You just want them to be illiterate and then get a job like me? Young man, why don't you just go back home and ask all your sisters if there is a woman happy being a bargirl."

I was appalled at her demeanour as she switched from calling me "darling" to "young man". Now I felt embarrassed.

That night stepfather and stepmother were waiting up for me when I arrived home. My stepfather spoke as soon as I entered the house.

"It's so late. Where have you been?"

I answered with the usual response: "My friends invited me to a party."

He spoke louder. "You're an adult now, huh? You work, get a salary, and spend it on dancing and drinking almost every night. I'm becoming increasingly annoyed with you."

I remained silent. Actually, I couldn't comprehend the reason for stepfather's anger. Then stepmother spoke.

"I heard that you scolded elder sister Keo. Is that right?"

When she reminded me about Keo, I glanced down at the floor and said nothing. Then stepmother approached me with fiery eyes and said, "Are you an animal or a human being? You have a job and a good salary. You dare to bum around and then despise your sister, huh?"

I answered her without admitting anything: "Stepmother, do you know what Keo does in public?"

She replied, eyes filled with tears: "I know! But just think. Don't you realise who she prostitutes herself for? Is she some goddess with magical powers to conjure money for you to spend frivolously? Could you and Moum have financed your university education alone? Could you have acquired the money to procure the necessary training needed for your great broadcasting job without her doing this? I don't think so."

I finally realised what Keo had done for Moum and me. The depth of her sacrifice shocked me, but I was still stubbornly insistent.

"You already knew about this? Our family used to have a good reputation. Everyone loved us, got along with us. Why didn't you stop her? Don't you know Moum and I don't want her doing this for us? Don't you realise how much we suffer from this shame?"

"You suffer!" she continued. "Don't I suffer? Doesn't Keo suffer? I couldn't get the money you needed for school. But your sister . . . she wanted you to study so you could have a great future. Do I have the right to stop her? You are her brother and sister. She does this for you, and then you say she's wrong. Please ask the bargirls around town if they have any problems. Do you think they are carefree? Did you ever hear Keo grumbling about her problems when she gave you money to spend heedlessly?"

Irritated, I walked to my room and slammed the door. I noticed the broken computer lying in the corner. I slowly sat down next to it, touching it gently, then felt some incipient emotion. In sorrow I remembered the day she had purchased this computer for me. She had brought it over with a beautiful smile and asked if it made me happy. I didn't realise what she'd had to do to buy it. Why did I get so angry yesterday and break it?

Actually, my stepmother is right. Whatever Keo did was for us. She didn't do anything wrong. I was the brute who dared to scold her.

I remembered the bag of snacks she had brought for us yesterday as she had done for many years. I pondered why, only yesterday, I demanded she throw them in the trash, and then I decided to find her.

I know self-forgiveness will be difficult. I just feel compelled to find her, to let her know she's a great person regardless of that profession. She is still noble, I still respect her. One day I hope to find Keo, to beg forgiveness for my cruelty. If I don't succeed, I may blame myself forever.

10

Nhem Sophath lives in Takeo province where he works as a teacher. "Lord of the Land" was awarded third place in short fiction at the Nou Hach Literary Competition, 2006. It was published in both Khmer and English translation in the Nou Hach Literary Journal, Vol. 6 (2006). This animal tale is about conflict between two herds of oxen, who maintained good relations when times were prosperous but became self-destructive, thoughtless, and brutal under external threat and diminished material well being. This is an allegory about the worst aspects of humanity under poverty and duress when even friends will turn upon each other.

Lord of the Land

Nhem Sophath

The sunlight is radiant. It is a wonderful day, which is why the wild oxen, the lords of the land, are so enthusiastic about life. The herd is happy because it is calving season.

One lord is standing near his wife, protecting her as she gives birth. He turns to look at another bull and jokes, "Laen! Your child looks like you; its body and face is so similar to yours. You must be skilful!"

Laen replies, "You are good too, Bouk! Your child is lovely and physically attractive. In the future these children will reproduce and continue our lineage."

"Yes, that is great," says Bouk. "Our children can do this."

While talking they move closer to Laen's wife. Her husband licks her affectionately and asks, "Dear, are you all right?"

"Yes, I'm fine," she says, while turning to observe the new-born calf as it attempts to stand, “but I’m tired. Our baby is so lovely. You must take good care of him.”

“I will.”

The wild ox herd is just like society; it has partisans, groups, and blocs. The oxen have divided themselves into two groups in this valley. The lord of one group is the biggest of the white ox group. They call him Laen. The lord of the other group is a stud bull. He is the biggest black bull. They call him Bouk.

Although they have different-coloured coats, Laen and Bouk accommodate each other. Each leads a group while being friends. They assist each other, recognising that they are all wild ox.

Time has passed. While they have been living in this valley, they could not plant rice or grow trees, so now they cannot find food easily. Before, the two groups had been living happily and peacefully, but now everything has changed.

The weather is extremely hot and all the land is parched because the climate is not the same. The grass in the meadows used to be so delicious, but the dry weather has made it like flavourless straw. There are wild dogs living at the base of one mountain now, and they always menace the herds. One by one the small calves are disappearing. On the other side of the valley at the base of the mountain is a river full of crocodiles. This river is the only source of water for all the oxen. The crocodiles conceal themselves to catch the oxen when they come to drink. One by one, many oxen have become crocodile food while others have been eaten by the wild dogs. Many die every day. They are living a miserable life with not enough food or water, and without any possibility of changing their location. These problems have caused the two herds to break off their friendship. They have split into many small groups, trying to find food and water.

Thirst and hunger have arrived in their world. Some of the members decide to search for food near the location of the wild dogs, even though they know it will be dangerous and they may die. Another small group conceals any food they find for themselves while another group goes far away to search for food.

Their life has become full of difficulty. They are cold, thirsty and hungry, making them all deceitful and intolerant. They stop being friends and decline to help each other. They cannot find any solution to these problems of survival. Even the two lords, who want their herds to live together, cannot solve these problems. This is such a sad situation. They cannot change anything. At this time every ox follows its own way.

The sun has set. Some oxen are walking to the river for water. Bouk's wife, at a distance from her husband, is also going there with their calf. She is talking to her child as they walk along.

"Child, please hurry up! The sun is setting."

"Mom, I'm still hungry," the calf replies as he stops to eat some grass. "What has happened to this place? There is no rain and there is not enough food. Some of us are even willing to risk death from the wild dogs to get enough to eat. Some have died."

The mother is happy when she realises her child is so insightful about their situation. Shortly, mother and calf arrive at the river and the calf sees another group of wild oxen eating young shoots. He goes to eat with them, but right before he reaches them, the ox called Adang lunges at him.

The calf tries to stand up, but he is hurt. Adang glares at him, shouting, "Hey, squirt! You know that this is my food."

The calf pleads, "I know it is yours but please give me some."

"What? Give you some? If I give it to you, I must be stupid."

Another ox in that group then threatens the calf. "You know, our land right now is so poor. There is no grass, nothing to eat. I'm almost dead from just trying to find food. Why are you asking for it? Just leave!"

No one is going to give the calf any food.

The hurt and frightened calf is crying out for his mother. She hears his cries and runs to him. When she arrives, she asks, "What happened?"

As the calf starts to reply, Adang interrupts. "His conduct was improper. Why is he so insolent, thinking that he can eat my food? A child like this should be disciplined."

Hearing this, the mother becomes angry since Adang is so disrespectful to her, the wife of the white lord of the land.

"You are insolent and overbearing! Why don't you respect my husband? He is the friend of your lord – "

Before she has even finished speaking, Adang shouts at her. "What respect? Nowadays, everyone just thinks for himself. It's different now. You must know this. Now we just need to survive. We don't care about idealism or laws or rules or human rights. We don't care. We just know that if we find food we eat it. We don't think about anything else. It's okay for you. Leave and take your child with you before I get angry and hurt you."

The mother doesn't understand how that small group could treat her like this.

"You ingrate!" she shouts. "You are not so great. Before when you had a problem, my husband helped you. Now you are ungrateful and look down on me. You don't even help my child! You are the new generation. You don't know the difference between good and bad actions. I'm civilised, but you are wild."

Adang replies, "Don't talk so much. Leave!"

"I'm not going anywhere. Do what you want to do to me," she replies in a worried voice.

The calf, perceiving the tension, walks underneath his mother, telling her, "Please stop. Let's go!"

"I'm not going anywhere. How can they treat us like this?" She starts walking toward Adang's group.

Adang glares at her and shouts, "Shut up! I can't restrain myself."

"Brother," says another member of his group, "she's crazy. We need to discipline her. Don't let her talk like this."

Another member of the group says, "Yes, I agree with you about her."

When Adang hears them respond like this, he gets even angrier, and starts to gore her with his horns. She fights back.

This anger is caused by starvation. Violence has destroyed their friendships and their ability to discern good and bad. All each wants to do is win. The calf stands nearby crying, wanting to stop Adang from goring his mother.

"Please stop, mother. Don't act like this," the calf shouts while running around them in circles.

This is a fight to the death. Suddenly there is a huge crash as the mother falls into the river, pushed by Adang, who then runs off with the rest of his group. They don't care about her being endangered by crocodiles.

The calf is crying when he sees that his mother has fallen into the river. He shouts for help. "My mum! Please help my mother!"

His mother tries to climb out of the river but her leg is trapped. In great pain, she shouts for help. "Help me, please help me!"

Her husband's group comes to help.

"Dear, please try to climb out!" her husband Bouk shouts as he rushes to help, but another member of his group stops him because the river is full of crocodiles.

"Don't go! Don't act like this. It is very dangerous," says Laan to Bouk.

"No! I have to help my wife. Please let me go." He struggles to get free.

None of the members in Bouk's group want to let him help his wife. She tries to free herself from the crocodile's grip but fails. She is now very tired. She sees her husband and child trying to help her, but says, "Stop! Don't come." She is being dragged into the river. As she watches them, she speaks her final words, "My dear, please take care of our child."

She is dragged under by a whole group of crocodiles while still trying to see her husband and child. Her husband stands by watching as his wife disappears under the water. He feels so sorry as he stands there in shock, thinking about the events of their life together. Their child is crying and shouting for his mother.

The father says, "My child, don't cry. Your mother has gone far away from us. We will never see her again." He licks the baby, trying to take care of him as tears stream down his own face.

Now the sun has set without concern for anything. The herd is returning to the valley.

It is a dark night and the herd sleeps, with the exception of Bouk and his child, who are thinking about what happened earlier that day. Bouk is crying alone, thinking fondly of his wife. Looking at the stars, he can't believe that she is dead. The entire night he thinks about why she died like this.

Finally Bouk wakes up his child to ask, "Little child, how did your mother fall into the river?"

"Dad," the child responds, still half asleep, "I know how!"

"Please tell me what happened."

The child tells his father what happened and Bouk is surprised to hear the word "fight". "What?" he says, "A fight! She was fighting for food? Humph. Why didn't they respect me? This is such a small thing. Why did Adang kill my wife? I must get my revenge."

Love, friendship, respect are all lost. At this time, all the oxen have revenge in their hearts. Bouk wants morning to come quickly so he can kill Adang.

Morning arrives and nature seems sad. The land is parched and all the animals are hungry. They hopelessly seek food in silence. This land that used to be so happy is now impoverished and getting worse. There are many wild dogs constantly threatening them now. The laws of this land are becoming less relevant day by day.

Bouk arrives at the black ox herd. Laan sees him arrive and says politely, "Oh, friend. Please come over here and eat with us."

Bouk replies, "I'm not coming to eat. I came to find out who killed my wife."

"What happened?" asks Laan. "Don't act like this."

Hearing this, Laan's herd stands around him and Laan's wife asks her husband, "My dear, what happened?"

"Don't worry," he replies, "he's coming for – "

"I did not come to be happy, or for a party, or to get food. I came to find justice for my wife!" Bouk yells.

Laan's wife attempts to comfort Bouk, saying, "Don't be angry. Your wife is already dead. You can't bring her back. You must be strong."

"My wife is not your relative, so it's easier for you to talk like that."

"Please don't act like this," interjects Laan.

Laan's wife gives advice, saying, "At this time, our situation is so bad. We don't think about personal things. We must find a solution for the entire group. Let's not ruin our friendship. As you know, the wild dogs are catching one of us every day. The crocodiles also. So right now we must stop and think about how endangered we are."

"I don't care about any of this. My wife was killed by a member of your group. So it's easy for you to talk like this. I must seek justice for my wife. Everything you say shows concern for the members of your group only."

"That's not so, but – "

"Don't talk so much! Please show me who killed my wife."

"Brother, I'd like to do that but I can't because he and his group were killed by wild dogs last night," Laan's wife replies.

"When you talk like this it means you want to keep it a secret."

"Oh, brother!" says Laan. "As she told you, they are all dead. I have no further information. If you don't believe me, please go seek the ghosts of the oxen in the wild-dog territory."

Laan leaves and Bouk chases after him, his old friend.

Laan's child yells to his father, "Watch out!" as he starts running in front of Bouk.

There is a crash and Laan and his wife are bewildered when they see their child fly up in the air and hit a tree, suffering a broken neck and lying motionless.

"Oh my god! Our child!" they exclaim.

Laan's group dashes to see what has happened to the child, who is already dead next to the tree. All the oxen in Laan's group are extremely sad, especially Laan and his wife.

What's done is done. The quarrel between the two groups has become very serious and difficult to resolve. Laan and his wife are crying and licking their dead child, missing him all ready.

"Oh child!" says the mother. "I really pity you. It's so sad you died so young."

Bouk just laughs. "Now you know how I feel?"

Bouk doesn't care about what happened to their child. He feels nothing.

"You are wild!" cries Laan. "Why didn't you listen to my explanation? You killed my child. Humph! At this time our herds cannot live together."

"You think I want to live together with you and your group?"

says Bouk. "All my feelings of friendship toward you left when my wife died. I will not be calm until I get my revenge."

"You must repay me for my child's life."

"Okay! We will see who is stronger!"

Hearing this, both herds run to fight. The situation is out of control between the two groups, making the valley tremble. The fight comes to a standoff and the herds separate.

After the fight, both groups have dead and wounded members. They destroyed the valley.

Now the herds are separated, dividing the land into two sections: one for Bouk's herd and one for Laan's. Dividing the vast empire was a disaster because there are enemies on all sides.

This morning, the grass is dewy and shimmering. In the dry season, the plants can grow from the dew that falls during the night. Bouk's herd found food at the base of the mountain but there is not enough. Suddenly there is a great commotion in the herd because the wild dogs are attacking. All of the oxen in Bouk's herd are trying to avoid the fangs of the wild dogs. Some are killed and others are wounded. Some are crying out for help. Bouk's child has been killed. Before the child died, he tried to shout to his father for help, "Father! Help me!"

After hearing this, Bouk gets up to fight the wild dogs and kills two or three of them. When the wild dogs see this, they shout for help. Then Bouk is killed by the wild dogs, following after his wife and child.

Bouk's herd separates and the wild dogs take control of their territory, expanding their empire. More and more wild oxen are killed each day.

The land becomes insecure. There is less food. Laan's oxen are very thin and weak. They cannot change their attitude, so Laan calls for a meeting to discuss their situation.

"You see what has happened. Right now our territory has become very dangerous. At this time, the pack of wild dogs is invading our land. We only have horns and we are weak. How can we protect our lives? So I think that we must leave here."

The sub-leader of the group asks, "Oh, leader, are you sure

you want to leave here? You won't regret protecting our heritage? Where should we go?"

"I know you are idealistic. No one wants to leave here, but you know this is a very difficult and dangerous situation. You see this. The land we control is shrinking. There is not enough food to eat and we are all very weak. Moreover, the herd is always fighting off the wild dogs and some of our members are wounded and crippled. Some die every day. If we stay here, there is only death by starvation or wild dogs."

All of the oxen in the herd listen to his explanation. But one of the thinnest oxen asks, "Oh leader, how can we leave this place? One side of the valley has a pack of wild dogs, the other side has a river with crocodiles. Another side has cliffs and we cannot cross."

Another ox, the leader of a faction within the herd, says, "We must take a chance. We had better not stay here just waiting to die."

Another ox says, "I think that we must stampede out of the wild-dog territory. This at least gives us some hope."

The leader of this faction says, "No, we shouldn't do that. We cannot cross the wild-dog territory because it's large. If we try to cross it, we will all die. There is only one way. We must leave across the river. We can have hope that way because the wild dogs cannot swim across and follow us."

An old ox says, "I don't agree. If we cross through the river, it's a gamble because there are crocodiles in the river."

The head of the faction replies. "How can we get free? If the river has crocodiles and the land route has wild dogs? If we continue to stay here we will die of starvation and the wild dogs will continue to threaten us. Our lineage will end here."

The old ox responds: "I won't be crocodile food. I'll leave through the wild-dog territory because we can try to fight off the dogs but we have no chance in fighting off a crocodile. Does anyone want to follow me? Let's go."

Laan says, "Stop! It's dangerous. Let's all agree on one plan and not divide into groups like this. What are you doing, proposing this?"

"Sorry! Now my group is separating from your leadership. Whoever thinks the way I do, comes with me."

In this disorder many oxen lose their conviction. They

Believe that the faction leader's conclusion is the best. They do not listen to Laan's objections.

The wild dogs are cruel as they mobilise to kill all the wild oxen of this faction as they try to escape across the wild-dog territory. They continue to penetrate Laan's territory.

Laan orders his herd to retreat to the edge of the river. There is no alternative. In front of them is the pack of snarling wild dogs and behind them is the river with crocodiles swimming in their direction. Laan has run out of ideas and says to the rest of the herd, "Everybody cross the river!"

The herd jumps into the river and makes the water turbulent. Some oxen escape the wild dogs, only to be devoured by the crocodiles. The sound of the water and the crocodiles killing the oxen is tremendous, with some oxen trying to escape their grip. Some cows try to swim to the shore.

No one can help anyone in this situation. Some wild oxen have good luck and are able to swim to the shore, while others get eaten. When some of the wild dogs reached the other shore, they are almost dead from exhaustion. The oxen are shouting to find their wives, husbands and children.

Laan is searching for his wife but he cannot find her. He knows clearly in his heart that his wife has not been able to cross the river. Tears stream down his face and he feels deep regret about everyone's loss of family and land.

The twilight has a melancholic feel. There is the sound of wild dogs howling, and there are many corpses of the wild oxen floating in the river. Laan, the lord of the white oxen, gazes at his lost land and leads some of the living oxen into the twilight.

11

Phou Chakriya is a young write who works as a journalist in Phnom Penh. "The Sun Never Rises" was awarded third place in short fiction at the Nou Hach Literary Competition, 2008. It was published along with an English translation in the Nou Hach Literary Journal, Vol. 5 (2008). The theme of grinding urban poverty dominates this story, a poverty compounded by the lack of opportunity to move up socially and economically without an education. The question of karma and compassion again arises in this story.

The Sun Never Rises

Phou Chakriya

I'm standing in front of an outdoor market looking around to see if anyone needs my services. It's approaching noon. I'm worried. I'm a cyclo-taxi driver. Every day, I work day and night, never resting. Otherwise, I would certainly have no food, and my wife and children would starve to death. I am watching Amao and Asok play at fighting, carefree about everything. These young men come from the provinces; they are about 20 years old. They don't care about making money. Although they have no customers, they ignore that. They are single and not like me, married with children.

Asok approaches me and asks, "What's up?"

"Nothing!"

"If so, why are you standing so stiff?"

I don't answer, but ask another question, "Buying a lottery ticket today?"

"Buy! My money is gone."

"Yes, go on gambling, you never know how to save money."

"Uncle! If I'm meant to be rich, I'll get rich."

"Hey, it's up to you to do it your way. Whatever you want to do, do it; but don't borrow my money. I have no money for you."

"You sound like you know me well," Asok starts massaging my shoulders.

"Yes, I know. I understand you so well."

"Uncle . . . !" Asok begs me, massaging my shoulders.

"Stop it," I say chasing him away, "you don't need to give me a massage. I have no money for you."

"Uncle! Don't be like that, just 5,000 *riels*."

"No, not even 1,000 *riels*."

"Oh, Uncle, please lend me some; I'll pay it back."

"Absolutely not! I haven't had a single customer this morning."

"Would you please forgive me for once . . . ," Asok starts to sing a song. I give him a gentle kick. He dodges it and then laughs.

"I'm older than you. You behave like this and you will fall into hell," I reprimand him.

"No, you're not old; you're still young."

I give him another kick, and he runs away laughing. I seem to be unreasonable with this young man. At that moment, a woman carrying many bags walks up to me and asks: "Will you give me a ride?"

"Yes, I'll take you!"

I go to help her with the bags and bring them to my cyclo.

"Please take me home," she says.

"Yes, Madam!"

I get on my cyclo, leave the market and head to her house. When I arrive, she takes money from her wallet and hands it to me for the ride. I take it and thank her.

I look at the lady's house. I see a big villa when they open the gate. I see three cars parked inside. Oh! She is so lucky, I think to myself. This woman is my steady customer; she always asks for my service to the market. She used to live in an apartment, but now she's moved up to this villa in just two years. Her life has changed in two years; as for me, I've been doing the same cyclo-driver job for the past twenty years.

I drive back to the market thinking, "Will I ever have the luck to live in a large house like that?" I take a deep breath. I'll only have it in my dreams.

At noon I come home to eat lunch with my wife and children. We sit together on a bed made of bamboo. I watch my children as they fight over food. We never have more than a couple of fish and some fish sauce. I look at my kids and pity them. They should not be born to such a poor father. What will their lives be like in the future? When I was young, I couldn't attend school due to poverty. When the country was at peace, I had no skills for work. That is why I became a cyclo-driver. I have no choice; I have to stay with this job in order to raise my kids. My life has been so unlucky. I can't swallow my food; I drop my bowl and walk inside.

"What's the matter?" my wife follows me inside.

"Nothing."

"If so, why did you stop eating?"

"I'm not that hungry. Leave the food for the kids. I'm tired and need a little rest."

I pick up a pillow to cover my face and lay on my bed. My wife doesn't say a word and walks out. I take the pillow off my face as she walks away. I look at the ceiling and start pondering. Other people have a wife and children. They possess cars, houses, and more money. My house is ugly like my clothes. They just relax and money comes to them. I run with my cyclo for money and still can't get enough. Although we are all born on the same earth, we're different. It is destiny. Others are wealthy because they must have great merit and this merit makes them rich. What little merit I have grows smaller and smaller. I don't know when I'll have good merit? Hey, the more I think, the more depressed I get. When will I be released from this karma? The more I think, the tougher my life feels. I take a deep breath and then sleep for a short while. I wake up and prepare to continue earning a living.

I've had just three customers for the whole evening. I count my money; it comes to only 4,000 *riels*. It is a small amount; yet Asok walks over, following me to ask about a loan.

"When I say no, I mean no. Go away!" I shout angrily at him.

"I only want to borrow 5,000 *riels*."

"I don't have that! I just have 4,000 *riels*. How can I find another 1,000 *riels* to lend? Stop bothering me. Go to Aphal; maybe he has it."

Even though I reproach him, he pays no attention and continues to bother me. I can't stand it. I get on my cyclo and head for home. If I stay there, I'll grow softhearted and lend him money. On my way back I find another customer. I'm happy thinking I can earn 1,000 or 2,000 thousand *riels* more.

"Where are you going, Ms.?" I ask her.

"To Sorya Market; how much do you charge?" she asks me.

"For one person?"

"Two—me and a child."

"Four thousand *riels*, Ms."

"Wow, that's expensive. How about 2,000 *riels*? It's not so far."

"Ms., it is far."

"Well, how about 2,500 *riels*?"

"Three thousand riels, please. There are two of you."

"Okay, let's go!"

After we agree on the price, we wait a moment for the child. Then I take both of them to Sorya Market and return home.

It's a silent night; my house has only one lamp. My children are sleeping quietly beneath a mosquito net. My wife is fanning them because it is the hot season and there is no breeze. I sit on the bamboo bed in front of the house and look at the waxing moon. My chest feels constricted so I take one deep breath for relief.

My wife approaches me, sits near, and asks: "Father, what are you thinking?"

"Nothing, nothing to do, just thinking," I reply.

"The light is getting dimmer. I think the battery is getting low," she says.

"It's okay. I'll take it to be recharged tomorrow."

"Our daughter has a cough. I want to take her to the doctor."

"Take her tomorrow, don't delay."

"But we don't have enough money . . . ".

"Go take it from my pocket. I earned over 5,000 *riels* today. Take it for her treatment."

My wife kept silent, and then she went inside the house to

bed. I sat alone for a moment then followed her.

The next morning I leave at dawn to take my wife and daughter to the doctor. After dropping them off at the clinic, I continue on to the market. I park my cyclo at the usual place and walk straight to my buddies. Asok, Amao, and Aphal are arguing and look like they have important issues to discuss.

I approach them and ask: "What's up? What are you talking about?"

"Nothing," Aphal answered. "What's wrong with you? Why are you here so early today?"

"Took my kid to see the doctor."

"What's wrong with your daughter?"

"She has a little cough . . . and what is your problem?"

"Um, yesterday I went to a pagoda. There is a monk who is good at giving lottery numbers. I went to get a number from him. Asok told me that he dreamed about number 25 last night, and that monk also gave me the number 25."

"It won't ever happen." I say, pursing my lips in disbelief.

"Well, sometimes it can happen, Uncle," Amao says defensively. "We humans can't predict our luck."

"Hmm, and what do you think?" I ask the group.

"I'm thinking; I don't know how much I should buy," Asok says.

"Eh, be thoughtful; I don't care. I'll warn you ahead of time not to believe in your dream. It can cause you to lose everything. Be careful!"

I stop talking then since a customer has called for me. I hurry to pick her up. When I come back, they have all disappeared. I am sure they have gone to purchase lottery tickets. Actually we know not to pin our hopes on winning at gambling. It's not easy to win, but it is the only way for poor people like us to get rich. I used to buy lottery tickets once in a while; but I found it to be useless and quit.

I've earned much more money than usual today so I come back home early in the evening. When I arrive home, my wife tells me that she needs to buy medicine. I give all of the money I've earned to her for this.

Early the next morning, I arrive at the market and see my three friends: "What's up! Which lottery number won?"

"We bought the number 25 but the winning number was 26. I'm so mad," Asok spoke angrily.

I laugh at him and say: "You see . . . you said that that monk was famous for giving the right lottery number; now, how is it?"

Asok replies: "Amao and I are fine; but Aphal . . . he spent all his rent money on the lottery. Now he doesn't have enough money to pay his rent."

"Is it true? So stupid!" I ask Aphal.

Aphal doesn't say a word and walks away. I don't know what to say to him and walk back to my cyclo. I'm afraid to ask him anything more. I had known the truth. Yesterday, I knew that the winning number was 26. I knew for sure that they had lost. I pretended to be a better person than they were but I'd also bought number 25 and lost with them. I think this is called bad luck.

The next morning I don't see Aphal at the market. I don't pay attention to his absence. At noon I go home to have lunch with my family as usual. When I return to the market, I see Amao and Asok.

They notice me and say: "Do you know, uncle? Aphal got hit by a car."

I am shocked when Amao tells me this and quickly ask: "How is he? What happened?"

"Because he lost the lottery, he didn't have the money for rent so he was working at night. Last night, he was driving a customer home. Suddenly, there was a car with a drunk driver. It hit him. I heard that now he's in the hospital."

"How do you know?"

"A lady who sells vegetables and lives close to his house told me," Asok explains.

"Is it bad?"

"Not so bad, I've heard."

"Hey, this is due to gambling. This is it. I'll wait to see if you'll all give it up or not?"

Asok and Amao kept silent.

When I get home, I lie down and start thinking to myself: Oh, god! What will happen to Aphal? He has no money and lost. How can he find the money for rent? His wife has no job; his children are still small. What will happen to his wife? I start thinking about my own life: one day, if I am not with my wife and five children, what will happen to them? It worries and frightens me.

There is an old proverb: "No one should be hopeless. Life is just like the sun; today, it sets, tomorrow it will rise so people should be hopeful." We should try hard to overcome obstacles; and one day, we will see the sunshine. I examine my own life over the past few years. It doesn't indicate any sign of hope. People say that we cannot know life's outcome; I really can't see any bright future for me. People say that, having gone through a dark night, the sun will shine tomorrow. Where was that light for me?

Three days have passed and Aphal is back to work. I notice that he looks extremely thin and pale. I ask about his situation. He tells me that his landlord will let him owe the rent; but he has to pay it by next month or get evicted. I look at him with sympathy but have no way to help him. I am also poor and work constantly to make my own living. I invite Aphal to eat lunch with me at my house because it is near and easy to get to. After lunch, he is in a hurry to get back to work in order to pay off his debt. I feel emotions for him, sad feelings because he is in the same situation as me. It's what they say: if life were supposed to be easy, we wouldn't be born as humans.

Today, I'm returning home earlier than usual; someone told me that my child is sick. When I get home, my wife tells me that my youngest one has a high fever. I quickly take my wife and daughter to the hospital. At the hospital I am very disappointed due to being poor. I try to find a doctor to check my kid but no medical staff will come. They leave us to wait so long. Finally they check her then give me a prescription. I don't know how to read and ask the doctor how to take the medicines.

"Don't you know how to read? They've written the explanation for you already."

"I'm illiterate; how can I read it?"

"Go to the pharmacy; they will tell you."

I have to pay for the examination and the prescription. The pharmacist speaks the same way as the doctor and the medical staff. I have heard it said that the hospital is a place to save human lives and that doctors are supposed to help people; but it wasn't like that. Don't bother to come see a doctor if you don't have money. The doctors and the hospital staff are scornful. When they see that we are poorly dressed, they ignore us. When we ask questions, they don't want to answer. Who said that doctors save lives? From my perspective, doctors turn life into death. I used all my earnings to buy medicine; it was really expensive. I take my daughter and wife home in silence.

The more I think, the more miserable I become. I didn't know how to get rid of this poverty. I look at the street and notice that young people are riding their motorbikes back and forth. They are born in a good time, to rich parents when the country is at peace. They never have to worry about money. Their food is expensive and nutritious; they have food left over to throw away. But for me, I can't even buy a big fish for a meal. I survive day to day just to subsist. I feel hopeless; perhaps my life will not get brighter.

Aphal sees me sitting alone; he walks over and asks: "How's your kid?"

"She's okay."

"Did you take her to the doctor?"

"Already!"

"What did the doctor say?"

"He said nothing, just prescribed some medicine."

"Hey, don't think so much! We were born with this fate. Don't be disappointed."

"No, I'm not disappointed, but . . . "

My throat tightens and it is difficult to speak.

Aphal lightly pats my shoulder and says: "Don't be disappointed with your destiny and don't complain about religion . . . we try, but are still poor. So, let it be."

"I wonder. After 1979 I've been working as a cyclo driver till 2000. Now I'm still a cyclo-taxi driver. That is what they call a life without achievement."

"Hey, why think this way? You know, the Buddha said that people are born with karma. People are born poor because of past sins. We have to accept our karma. Some people say that if we ever produced good merit in the past, it would help us; but it will come when it is the right time. We must be patient, my friend! Maybe when your children grow up, they will be able to help you. Or they'll have good merit. They will become rich. On that day, you will be removed from this poverty."

I listen to Aphal, what he said about my children. I have five children and the eldest one is just about seven years old and I'm forty. By the time they are successful, I'll be under dirt. Then how could I use their money? Oh god, please notice me. It's not only me; there are many Cambodians living in this condition. Why don't you save us? Are you going to come after we are dead?

Aphal leaves to assist a customer. I also have one.

"How much do you charge to Samthaumuk School?" an old woman asks me.

"Three thousand *riels*, Auntie?

"Oh, so expensive! Two thousand *riels*, okay?"

"No, from Depo Market to Santhaumuk, it's not expensive at this price."

"For 2,000 *riels*, I'll go. That's how much I pay every day."

After thinking for a moment, I agree. I drive to her house and she pays me. After getting my money, I raise my hand to turn my cyclo back to the market. While I'm turning in the middle of the road, I'm struck with a loud bang. Thrown from the cyclo, I fall to the pavement at the side of the road. Panicked people are all around me and I hear many voices.

"What happened to him? Help him, please!"

"What's the problem? Who hit him?"

"A Land cruiser, hit-and-run . . ."

"Help him? How is he?"

"How did the Land cruiser hit him?

"He was turning the cyclo. A Land cruiser was driving too fast and hit him."

"Call an ambulance. Help him for merit. He should be pitied."

I open my eyes slightly and see a lot of people gathered around me but their images are blurred. I try to open my eyes again. The sunlight shining on me is growing dimmer and dimmer . . . .

12

This short story, from a collection of short fiction by Sok Chanphal, was translated by Yin Luoth in 2009. It is distinguished by its existential, reflective quality.

The Last Part of My Life

Sok Chanphal

One afternoon, I was strolling on the beach and met a man around thirty years old, who was sitting and painting under a pine tree whose branches danced along with the waves and their sound. In his painting there were multicolored clouds and the sea at sunset. He painted like a real skilled, professional painter, but his painting was not beautiful. It was similar to a child's painting in the purest and honest sense.

He asks me, "Do you think it is beautiful?"

I answer smiling, "It looks like a kid's painting."

The man continues to dip his brush into some red color to paint a big sun among the clouds. Then he continues to ask me, "Do you think the sun is too big or too small?"

I answer, "Too big. It is really big."

Each time he speaks, he never turns to look at me. He continues saying, "I like the sunset. That is why I paint it big."

"It doesn't look natural," I answer.

"It doesn't look natural, but it is natural."

After this response, he turns to look at me. His eyes look gentle under thick eyebrows. He smiles and with a tender sigh asks,

"Do you have a happy life?"

I look at the painting while ignoring his question.

He continues. "What do you think? I think, this world is a laughing stock . . . hard workers get tired while lazy people have easy lives; smart people end up with misfortune while ignorant people become fortunate . . . good people are violated by bad people while doing a good deed ends up with a bad result. Serious people are controlled by sloppy ones . . . good savers have to turn money over to loose spenders. Persistent people continue to persist . . . . Without cancer, I'd have to work hard until the day I die."

I ask him, "You have cancer?"

"Right," he smiles, "but you don't need to be sympathetic because I am the most happy, sick person."

"Why?"

"Cancer destroys my future. It gives me the full meaning of the present. You can see that right now I have full freedom. I sit and paint anything I want without having to worry about whether it's good or if I have to please somebody?"

"Why is this? Because you are sick?"

"Because this sickness allows me to do what I like during the last part of my life, to be whomever I want. When I didn't know that my life was coming to an end, I had to work hard. I tortured myself from childhood. I studied hard. It almost caused a nervous breakdown. I misled myself. I've never done anything for me. I like to read novels for pleasure, but I thought it was not as useful as reading textbooks. I like to listen to music, but I pushed myself to listen to the news."

When he says this, I laugh. He pats my shoulder, asks me to sit, and continues to question me, "Do you think this life is only about persistence?"

"Not true. I think life is about hope."

He was quiet for a moment and then said, "Actually my life is good. I sleep as much as I want. I can take a stroll. I do what I want. No pressure in my life. Must I also have hope? Must I?"

81201959R00059

Made in the USA
Lexington, KY
13 February 2018